OCT 2022

MCSEA BOOKS
www.mcseabooks.com

Publisher's Cataloging-in-Publication Data
provided by Five Rainbows Cataloging Services

Names: Cocca-Leffler, Maryann, 1958- author, illustrator.
Title: Heart stones / Maryann Cocca-Leffler.
Description: Lincoln, ME : McSea Books, 2022. | Summary: Gale and
Celia solve a missing sailors mystery after heart-shaped stones appear
and strange magical events happen. | Audience: Grades 3-8.
Identifiers: ISBN 978-1-954277-03-8 (softcover) | ISBN 978-1-954277-
02-1 (hardcover)
Subjects: LCSH: Illustrated works. | CYAC: Magic--Fiction. | Maine--
Fiction. | Hope--Fiction. | Natural disasters--Fiction. | Detective and
mystery fiction. | BISAC: JUVENILE FICTION / Mysteries & Detective
Stories. | JUVENILE FICTION / Fantasy & Magic.
Classification: LCC PZ7.C638 He 2022 (print) | LCC PZ7.C638 (ebook) |
DDC [Fic]--dc23.

Printed in the United States of America

Designed by Jill Weber
Text set in Charlotte Std

Heart Stones

Maryann Cocca-Le[

McSea Books

To my family—
Eric, Janine, and Kristin,
who happily walk the beach with me,
searching for heart stones.
Thank you for your love and support.
Love, M

The afternoon sky was as dark as the inside of my closet, and the low tide made it sort of smell like my closet too. The snow piles on the edge of the school-yard were now clumps of black, filthy ice, slowly melting, turning our soccer field to mush. March. Mud season in Maine.

Finally, my sister Emma walked out the double doors. She paused, looked up, and pulled her hood over her long curly hair. Her face looked as gloomy as the sky.

"I hate group projects," Emma said. "Sophie's such a slacker. She didn't even pass in her tide chart."

Our Friday afternoon walk to the LaundromArt turned into a poorly choreographed puddle dance, with Emma doing the stomp while I did the tippy-toe side step. Most days a stroll down Shore Drive was like walking through one of those idyllic Maine calendars, but not today. The narrow street was crowded with big noisy trucks. A loud banging vibrated from the water. We blocked our ears.

"What's that giant machine doing in the harbor?" I screamed.

"They're fixing the dock!" Emma yelled. "The storm wiped it out—remember?"

Of course, I remembered. No one in Cliff Cove will ever forget the Valentine's Day nor'easter that destroyed our community. Mom said it was the worst storm to hit our seaside town in a decade…and believe me—my mom knows storms. Last month, on my birthday, I had to listen to the story again: *Ten years ago today you were born in a blizzard…* Well, actually, I was born in a snowplow on the way to the hospital in a blizzard. My parents named me Gale Hope: Gale, because they said I came into the world like a big gust of wind, and Hope, because that's what everyone needed at the time.

Looking around, I'd say we could all use a little hope just about now. Four short weeks ago, the storm blew in, leaving the entire town in one big mess.

We cut through the Town Green, which buzzed with the sound of chain saws. Bright orange caution tape surrounded a big oak tree, its huge limbs damaged by the storm.

"Our climbing tree. I can't believe it's being cut down," I said.

"I can't believe the statue survived!" said Emma.

We looked up the path. There, the bronze fisherman statue stood alone, like a boat in a big sea. The melting snow revealed a mound of wilted flower bouquets at its granite base. The sight of the flowers brought us back to that cold February night. The entire town had gathered on this exact spot for a candlelight vigil to honor the two lobstermen lost at sea during the storm.

We walked closer and spotted our card, sopping wet, still attached to the bouquet, now a sad-looking bunch of soggy dead roses.

"My watercolor painting of a rainbow turned all gray," I said.

Emma gently peeled open the card. The message had been washed away, but we could still make out the date, February 22nd.

That was the saddest night ever.

We continued toward Main Street, where the shops were waking up like hibernating bears after a long cold winter. The shredded, red awning at Scoops Ice Cream was being replaced, this time with blue-and-white stripes. New signs were being hung, windows unshuttered. Everyone was working to get Cliff Cove ready for the summer season.

As we rounded the corner to the LaundromArt, we almost bumped into Sam. He was in front of Joe's Market, hunched over, seriously strumming his guitar. His music was drowned out by the sound of a barreling truck hauling sand toward the harbor.

"Hey, Sam!"

He nodded, not missing a beat. I looked down. A few coins dotted his open guitar case.

"It's official. Spring is on the way," Emma said.

This was Sam's corner. Like a migrating bird, he showed up in Cliff Cove every year as soon as the snow began to melt and stayed until the first autumn snowflakes.

A gust of warm air hit our faces as we entered the LaundromArt, immediately fogging up my eyeglasses with a blur of wild color. I wiped my glasses on the bottom of my sweatshirt and refocused on the massive mural. This wasn't your average laundromat; it was Anna's LaundromArt, Mom's creation, one part laundromat and one part art studio. Where else can you do your laundry, sip a cappuccino, see an exhibit, and learn printmaking? It's also where Emma and I go almost every day after school to help out and do our homework.

We stashed our backpacks and jackets under the counter and stole chocolate candies from the bowl. Emma whipped out her calculator, grabbed the folder next to the cash register, and headed for the back office to add up the receipts.

Mom gave a quick wave. She was helping Captain organize the laundry for today's delivery. Captain, a tall rugged man with a gentle smile, is Mom's one and only employee. Typically, Captain worked part-time during the slow winter months, but this has not been a typical winter. Mom, Captain, and the six washing machines have been working overtime, and today was no different.

I listened to the familiar melody of the machines, humming and whirring. The place was busy. Lots of residents still didn't have power. I looked around and spotted Mr. Chin folding a pile of tiny clothing as his toddler wrapped her arms around his knees. Lilly, our neighbor, was rocking to tunes from her earbuds as she waited for her laundry to dry, while in the corner, *Cliff Cove Times* reporter and busybody Edith Styles was sipping coffee, engrossed in a book, with her feet propped up on an empty laundry basket.

Mom walked toward me with an armful of clothes.

"Okay, deliveries are set. I'm telling you, Gale, it's busier than ever. Everyone is packing up winter." With a grunt, Mom tossed a pile of coats on the counter.

I knew what that meant. Pocket time. My job, the job nobody wanted, was to empty the pockets before the clothes went to dry cleaning. I tried to make it fun by making a mystery game out of it. I love mysteries. I would close my eyes, feel something in the pocket, and try to imagine what it was before I pulled it out. I learned the hard way that it was a good idea to wear disposable gloves. People leave disgusting things in their pockets. One time, I imagined a big lump in a kid's coat pocket was a small cute stuffed animal. Nope. I pulled out a slimy dead frog. Yuck.

I felt around the pockets and silently guessed the usual stuff. I was right. I pulled out…wads of tissues, a half stick of gum, small pieces of sea glass, a shell, and lots of loose coins. Anything that was worth keeping I'd put in small envelopes to be returned to the owner.

Just then, the bell over the door jingled. I turned, expecting a customer, but it was just Sam. He's a regular at our "complimentary coffee" counter. Today he was smiling, and Sam never smiles.

"Look what I found in my guitar case!" he said, holding out his hand in front of my face. In it was a smooth, glistening, reddish-pink stone.

"Wow, that's amazing. It's shaped like a perfect heart!" I said.

Sam beamed. "I've been playing on that corner

for years, and I was pretty sure that no one was even listening. Well, someone is listening! And they love my music."

"Did you see who tossed it in your case?" I asked.

"No. I left for a minute to go into Joe's Market, and when I came back, it was there."

"Can I hold it?" I took off my plastic gloves and Sam dropped the heart-shaped stone into my hand, then sauntered over to the coffee counter. I examined it closely. Mom and I have been collecting heart-shaped beach stones for years, but this was different. The color was like nothing I had ever seen. I held it up to the window. It glowed. I rubbed it gently. Suddenly, a warm peaceful sensation traveled up my arm and settled in the middle of my chest.

Just then, Emma came from the back office. I held up the stone.

"Emma, you have to check out this stone!" I said, offering it to her. "Here, hold it in your hand."

"Why?"

"I don't know. It's weird. I rubbed it and felt this warm tingling feeling up..."

"Static electricity," Emma said flatly.

I groaned. Everything with Emma had to be explained by science.

"No—really—I think..." I gave up trying to explain and walked over to Sam, who was now balancing a cup of hot chocolate.

"That's cool, Sam." I handed him the stone, looking at it one more time.

"Keep that stone," I told him. "It could be lucky."

I heard Emma groan. "Ohhh—maybe it's magic!" she teased in a singsongy voice.

I ignored her. She has no imagination. I put the coats on a rack, rolled them to the back room, and grabbed the mail.

"Mom, I'm heading to the post office," I called.

TWO

Once again, I cut through the Town Green, this time passing a freshly cut tree stump. The buzz of the chain saw had been replaced by the scrape of rakes.

As I passed the fisherman statue, something caught my eye. I stopped. The wilted flowers were gone, and in their place were beautiful bouquets with perfectly formed yellow ribbons.

I smiled. I thought it was cool that someone left fresh flowers. I wandered over to take a closer look. That's when I saw it, a familiar bouquet, our bouquet, with a card. *Our card!*

"It can't be," I whispered.

I squatted down. My watercolor rainbow was no

longer a blended, soggy gray but vivid colors, the way I'd painted it nearly three weeks ago on the day of the candlelight vigil. I opened the card. This time I could read the entire message, our signatures, and the date. I blinked hard, shook my head, and adjusted my glasses. I took the card off the fresh bouquet of red roses and examined it again, closely.

"This can't be real," I said.

I slipped the card into my jacket pocket and began to read the other cards, all dated February 22nd, all crisp and dry, just like the day they were placed there. My eyes watered as I remembered that night. Seeing Josie and her family huddling in sadness was heartbreaking. Her brother Carlos was only nineteen. He had just started working on Pierre DuPont's fishing boat last summer. Pierre. Everyone knew Pierre. He had been fishing in Cliff Cove forever. Both of them, gone. Just like that. Stupid storm.

Since then, a cloud of gloom had hung over the town. I saw it every day on Captain's face. Pierre had been Captain's closest friend and fishing buddy. Smiles waned everywhere: at the fishing pier, the bookstore, and the ice cream shop. Even the yellow ribbons in the store windows were starting to fade, and with them, hope.

I blinked away my tears.

That's when I saw them—two pink, glistening heart-shaped stones, balancing on the edge of the statue's granite base.

When I got back to the LaundromArt, it was almost closing time. Emma was on the couch reading. I patted my jacket, feeling the lumps of the stones and card. I was just about to tell Emma what I found at the statue but stopped. Emma would never believe me. Now if Kayla were here, she would be so excited. I missed Kayla. That storm took away a lot of things, including my best friend. Her whole family had to pick up and move to Portland while their house was being fixed.

One by one, I turned off all the lights as Mom cashed out the register. We grabbed our backpacks and shuffled outside.

"Okay, girls, let's run home and have a quick dinner," Mom said as she locked the door. The Friday evening dash began. Mom needed to get back by seven o'clock for her painting class.

"Where's that music coming from?" Mom asked, looking around.

I glanced to the corner. "It's Sam," I said.

"Sam? Can't be Sam. It sounds too good," said Emma.

It *was* Sam. For the first time ever, he was actually attracting a small crowd. People were swaying to the music. Sam, head bopping, strummed his guitar as he sang loud and clear.

"Wow. Impressive," said Emma. "He must have taken some serious lessons over the winter."

I looked at Sam. He had changed. His music had changed. His voice was amazing. It wasn't lessons. I felt for the heart stones in my pocket.

The March sun was setting as we walked the three blocks to our house. I loved living downtown. I walked everywhere, especially in summer when it stayed light till eight-thirty. But the bad part was, when summer arrived, so did a zillion tourists who invaded the town like hungry ants. There was always a downside.

We took a turn onto our street, Higgins Road, passing a line of white houses with black shutters. Then, *bam*, like a lit Christmas tree in the desert, our yellow house popped into view. As we climbed the porch, Mom stopped at the empty flower boxes.

"I can't wait till spring," she sighed.

Mom says there is no such thing as too much color or too many flowers. Soon, the empty flower boxes would be bursting with pink petunias and the front yard jam-packed with red roses and blue hydrangeas. Inside, our home was filled with art: paintings, pottery, weavings, and sculptures were everywhere. Some were Mom's creations, some bought in galleries, and others were thrift store finds. It was like living in our own mini-museum.

We hurried to get dinner on the table. I stared at the leftover chicken cacciatore and moved the peppers to the side with my fork. Not my favorite.

"Okay, girls, let's catch up before I have to dash back to the studio," said Mom. "How was school?"

Emma told Mom about her disappointing grade on her science project.

"Emma, don't worry. Mrs. Thompson knows exactly who's doing the work," said Mom. "It will be fine."

Then Mom turned to me. "Gale, you're so quiet. What's going on?"

"Tell Mom about the magic stone!" Emma teased.

"Stone? What stone?" asked Mom.

"It was nothing," I mumbled.

"Really, I want to hear about it. What stone?" Mom asked again, curious.

"Well, Sam showed me a stone in the shape of a perfect heart," I began.

"We've found a ton of heart-shaped stones on the beach," Mom said. "Was it unusual?"

"Very. This was different." I paused, trying to think of how to explain, without sounding zany. "Well, it was sort of a glowing, pinkish-red color, and when I rubbed it, I felt, like, this strange tingling down my arm…"

Emma crossed her arms and rolled her eyes.

I continued, "And then this afternoon, at the fisherman statue, I saw something… umm, something, well, unbelievable…"

Mom looked at her watch, smiling. "Gale, you *are* a dreamer."

"That's what I said, Mom," Emma chimed in.

"Gale, tell me the whole story tomorrow. I really have to run." Mom piled the plates on the counter, gathered her bag, and dashed out the door.

As I watched her leave, I thought about the two heart stones and the rainbow card tucked safely in the top drawer of my dresser.

I wasn't dreaming.

ad came to pick us up at eight o'clock on Saturday morning. It was Maine Maple Weekend, and he had the entire day planned. He pulled out the map.

"Ready, girls? We're hitting every sugar shack from here to Acadia. First stop—Charlie's Maple Barn."

"I need a few minutes." Emma ran down the hall.

I took off my glasses, threw on my favorite Red Sox sweatshirt, and pulled my striped knit hat over my short wavy hair. "I'm ready. Maine blueberry pancakes, here we come!"

I could get ready in two seconds flat, but not Emma. Mom calls her "the organizer extraordinaire." I call her "slow as molasses." She can't leave the house unless everything is just so. She even lines up her shoes. We are sisters, but we are total opposites. We don't even look alike. Emma looks like Dad. She's got the Henderson hair and height, shiny auburn curls, and slim, long legs. Me, I'm all Tremonte. Just like Mom, I have dark brown, wavy hair and olive skin. When I look at Mom, I see my future, a five-foot-three Italian beauty. I'll take it.

Dad and I waited at the table. My stomach rumbled. Finally, Emma came out of the bathroom with perfectly braided hair and a sweater that matched her socks. Who does that? We all grabbed our coats and boots and headed out the door.

"Have a great time, girls. Bring me back two jugs of maple syrup—the big size," said Mom.

We slid in the front seat of Dad's old green pickup truck, me in the middle. I knew enough not to mess with the radio station. It's country music the whole way. We headed north singing along to Dad's favorite tunes.

Charlie's was packed. We parked at the edge of the field and slopped in our rubber boots through the muddy parking lot to the Barn. We entered the restaurant and spotted an empty bench at a long wooden table in the corner.

"Hey, Barb!" called Dad as we all settled in.

"Hi there, Ben. Gale, Emma…how's my girls?"

Barb poured Dad coffee and served us orange juice. She took the pencil from behind her ear and posed with her notepad.

"Specials on the board," she said, winking. "But I know you girls, and you aren't interested in any ol' spinach omelet. Are ya?"

"No…we want…"

"I've already got it down." Barb smiled. "Three big ol' stacks of blueberry pancakes coming up with…"

"Maple syrup," we said together.

"Make that Grade A," added Emma.

"You got it, sweet things!"

Dad laughed as Barb marched to the kitchen. "We may need a new breakfast spot. We'll never be able to order anything *but* blueberry pancakes!"

"Luckily, we love them!" Emma said.

Charlie's is our go-to place for breakfast on Saturdays, but sometimes Dad makes us breakfast at his place. His specialty is French toast. Dad's apartment is in the next town on South Harbor. He lives above Mac's Fish and Tackle Shop on the pier. It's a little cramped and a bit stinky, but you can't beat the view. Dad works as a computer programmer for some tech company, but lately he's been spending a lot of time helping Mac repair the Tackle Shop, which got hit pretty hard in the storm.

We've been spending Saturdays with Dad for as long as I can remember. When I was three years old and Emma was five, Mom and Dad split up. Mom says they "fell out of love." I'm not sure how that happens, but I still like to hear the story of how they fell *IN* love.

They both went to college in Boston, Mom in art school, Dad studying computers. They met in a dingy country music bar outside of Fenway Park. When Mom tells the story, she says Dad was pretty hard to miss. She spotted a tall, out-of-step country line dancer, moving in the wrong direction. When Dad tells the story, he says he noticed this pretty lady, with a wild-colored dress, staring at him and was convinced that his dancing skills lured her in.

Either way, they soon discovered they were both city-haters-out-of-staters, Mom from New Hampshire and Dad from Tennessee. They escaped the city every chance they could, most times heading up to Maine to camp under the big pines or walk the rocky shores. They fell in love with Maine and each other. And here we are.

After stuffing ourselves with pancakes, we walked up the hill to the Sugar Shack and Store. Sweet-smelling steam bellowed out of the chimney. Dad waited outside, examining one of the old rusty antique tractors. We entered the Shack, where a small group of people were listening to Eddie explain the maple syrup process. Four little kids with sticky fingers were only focused on eating their maple donuts.

I looked down at their Nike sneakers covered with mud.

"They're not from Maine," I whispered to Emma. "Anyone from Maine knows to wear waterproof boots in March. Where do you think they're from?"

"Who are you? FBI? Who cares?" Emma said.

"I'm guessing Massachusetts. That lady has a Boston University hat on."

"Can we focus on getting Mom her syrup?" asked Emma.

We made our way to the back shelves, grabbed two big jugs of maple syrup, and paid the cashier.

When we got into the car, Emma held up one of the jugs. "It took twenty gallons of sap to make this half gallon of syrup. When you boil the sap, the water evaporates. The darker the color the stronger the flavor…"

Emma continued with the science lesson. I had tuned her out about three minutes earlier when she said the words *reverse osmosis*. She loves the science behind syrup. I just like to eat it.

After two more maple sugar shack stops, including a live outdoor country music concert and a hot air balloon ride, we arrived in Ellsworth for the Maine Maple Festival. We spent the rest of the day at the fairgrounds, playing games and going on rides. I mostly stuck to the games. Spinning rides made me too woozy, and I wanted to make sure I saved my stomach for our last stop, Mrs. Fritz's famous apple maple ice cream. Yum.

On the long car ride home, Emma fell asleep. Yes! We didn't have to listen to her tell us all about the science of hot air balloons, which earlier she promised to explain.

"Hey, Dad. Do you believe in magic?"

"What do you mean?"

"Can a stone be magic?"

"A stone? What kind of stone?"

I told Dad all about the heart stones and about the flowers and the card. Surprisingly, he didn't laugh at me or call me a dreamer.

"Are you sure it was the same card?" Dad asked. "Could someone be playing a trick on you?"

"No, Dad. The flowers and the cards…they were all fresh, like on the day of the vigil," I said.

"Tell you what, how about I go check out the Town Green and take a look at those flowers?"

"Okay. Can we go now? On the way home?" I asked.

"Sure."

"Let's drop Emma off first," I whispered. "She thinks I'm loopy."

We pulled up to our house. Emma stumbled sleepy-eyed out of the truck, carrying the two jugs of syrup. She turned and watched with a confused look as I closed the truck door.

I rolled down the window. "We'll be right back. Just need to run to the store," I said.

Dad parked at the Town Green. The sun was setting and our long shadows led the way up the path, straight toward the fisherman statue. I looked down at the base. There was nothing there.

"They must have taken everything away. The flowers…they were here yesterday."

"Now, Gale."

"Really, Dad. I can prove it. I have the card and the stones. They're in my dresser."

I could tell he didn't believe me.

"Let's go home. I'll show you."

We crept into the kitchen. It was quiet. Mom wasn't home and Emma was in her room. I went straight to my dresser and got the stones and card.

Dad examined the heart stones. "Wow. They *are* beautiful—perfect heart shapes, but not identical." Dad looked closer. "Mmmm, the color is similar and both stones have gold specks, but I think…"

Before he could continue, I handed him the card. "See, it's dated February 22nd, the night of the candle-light vigil."

"Gale, I think someone is making these stones in a shop or something. Maybe it's some kind of marketing stunt."

"Marketing stunt for what? What about the card? And the fresh flowers?"

"Maybe the card dried in the sun after the snow melted," said Dad. "Maybe someone replaced those flowers. You have to be rational. There's got to be some kind of logical explanation."

I sighed.

It looked like I'd have to solve this mystery on my own.

FOUR

O n Monday, I saw Celia passing around something at
the lockers and heard lots of "oohs" and "ahhs." My
eyes followed the object as it went from Emir to Josie,
who examined it closely and then passed it back to Celia.

"My sister Angela, who works at the Dolphin Diner,
found it in the tip jar on Saturday," said Celia, "and then,
the craziest thing happened…"

I wiggled my way into the circle and then I saw it. It
was another heart stone.

Celia continued, "Okay, so Angela takes the stone out
of the jar and shows it to her boss. He picks it up. Then
all of a sudden, he smiles and yells out, *"Fish chowder for
everyone—on the house!"*

"But what's so crazy about that?" Emir asked.

"Have you ever met Mr. Wheeler? He is the grumpiest, stingiest man in town. He never gives anything away!"

"And he's not good to the fishermen either," said Josie. "He always wants the cheapest price and then never pays them on time. Carlos was always complaining about him."

The mention of Carlos brought a brief awkward silence. I was so sad for Josie, but in these moments, I never knew what to say.

Celia gave Josie a little hug, then continued, "I know. My sister complains about him too. That's why it's so weird. It's like, all of a sudden, he got nice. So anyway, word got out about the free chowder, and all the wait-staff worked nonstop till closing. Angela figured that the fish chowder would run out sooner or later, but it never did. She said it was like a magic pot that had no bottom. Isn't that nuts?"

I squeezed next to Celia, getting a better look at the stone.

"Sam found a heart stone just like that in his guitar case on Friday," I said.

"Are you kidding?" Celia looked at me. "The same shape and color and everything?"

"Yup. Same. Did Angela see who dropped the stone in the jar?" I asked.

"She doesn't have a clue. Whoever it was, I have to

thank them. I think this little rock has some big powers! Maybe there are more heart stones out there."

I was going to mention the two stones that I found at the fisherman statue, but when I looked at Josie and thought about her brother, I couldn't.

I just shrugged.

It was hard to focus in English class. I stared at the handout and started doodling around the edge of the paper. Mr. Elliot was telling the class all about our next writing project.

"Pick an author and read two of their books. There's a list of suggested authors on page two. Research the author's life and write a biography, then try to connect their life to their books. Be a detective. Ask questions like *Why did they pick their topic? Was there something in their life that sparked the idea?*"

My ears perked up at the word "detective."

"Can we do an oral presentation?" asked Collin.

Collin was into acting.

"That's a great idea, Collin. Yes. You can talk about your author. If you dress up as your author, you'll get extra credit."

A few kids cheered, including Celia. Not me. I didn't like talking in front of the class or dressing up in anything other than jeans and a sweatshirt. I thought about Mr. Elliot's words: "Be a detective. Ask questions." That's what I liked. I looked at my doodles, all hearts and question marks. I had a lot of questions, that was for sure:

Why are these stones showing up in town?

Where are they coming from?

Who is handing them out? Why?

At lunch, I sat in my usual spot at my usual table, leaving space for Kayla. Then I remembered. Kayla was a hundred miles away eating lunch at a new school with her new friends. Celia was examining her heart stone while flipping open her yogurt. She looked at me, looking at her.

"Who are you picking for your author?" she asked.

"Not sure yet." I unzipped my lunch bag, wondering what Mom packed today.

"What about going to the library after school? Maybe we can get inspired," Celia suggested.

"Today?" I looked up at Celia, then at the empty seat between us.

"Yes. If you want to," said Celia.

"Okay, sounds good." I took a bite of my sandwich. It was hummus with sprouts. It looked like Mom was on a health food kick again. I sipped my milk as I watched Celia spin the heart stone on the table. The color of the stone matched the dribble of raspberry yogurt on her shirt. "I think I might pick a mystery writer, maybe Mildred Benson," I said.

"Good idea. Maybe if we read mysteries, we'll figure out our own mystery."

I stopped. Did I hear that right? Did she just say *our* mystery? I put down my half-eaten sandwich and turned to Celia. "So, *you* think this heart stone thing is a mystery too?"

"Well, it's something." Celia picked up the stone. "I think this little heart changed Mr. Wheeler's heart and fed a whole lot of people. Someone has to be handing out these heart stones. You said Sam found one? I'll bet there are more out there."

I looked around the table and saw that Collin, Emir, and Tory were engrossed in their own conversation. I scooted closer to Celia, right over invisible Kayla, and said softly, "Yes…there are more."

With wide eyes, Celia leaned in. "What do you mean?"

"I found two heart stones on Friday," I whispered.

"You what?" Celia blurted out. The kids at the table looked at us.

I put my finger to my lips. "Not now. I'll tell you on the way to the library."

FIVE

At the end of the day, I found Celia in the hallway, struggling to dislodge her coat from her locker. Lots of stuff tumbled out.

"How do they expect us to fit everything in here?" Her long straight dark hair covered her face as she squatted to retrieve her treasures.

I shrugged.

Celia's locker was packed. The inside of the door was plastered with Broadway playbills, photos, and a yellowing school newspaper clipping with the headline WIZARD OF OZ—FALL PRODUCTION—CELIA SHEN PLAYS DOROTHY. I picked up a sparkling red shoe from the floor. Celia tossed it in her locker and slammed the door shut with her hip. Our minds were on something else sparkling and red: heart stones. We walked down the hallway, our eyes dancing a knowing look.

Outside, I met up with Emma at our usual spot in front of the middle school. "Tell Mom I'm going to the library. I'll be at the LaundromArt by four o'clock."

"Okay, Gale. But I'm not doing all your work," Emma said with a huff. "I have a ton of homework." She hoisted her backpack over her shoulder, turned, and headed down Shore Drive. Celia and I headed in the opposite direction toward the library.

As soon as we were a safe distance from the school, Celia turned and said, "Spill it! What stones? You have to tell me everything!"

And I did. I told her all about the two stones I found at the base of the fisherman statue and the magical transformation of the wilted flowers and cards.

Celia stopped in her tracks and looked at me, her jaw hanging open. "Gale, this is big. I knew it!" Her booming dramatic voice was attracting attention from a group of kids across the street.

"Shh," I tried to hush her.

"Oh, sorry. I know, backstage voice." She leaned in. "These stones are not your average rocks. We have to find out who is leaving them around town and why."

"So, you believe me then?" I was relieved.

"Why wouldn't I? Wait. Are you making this up?" Celia said.

"No, no. It's true, all true. It's just that my family thinks I'm imagining things, especially my sister."

Celia took the stone out of her pocket. "How can she not believe you? *This* is real! Not imagined. I'm telling you—this stone has some kind of magic power. When I rub, I…"

"You get a tingling warm feeling?"

"How did you know?"

"Because I felt it too," I said. "Maybe it's giving off some kind of energy, like positive energy or something. Every time a stone shows up, it seems like good things happen: like Sam's new attitude, the flowers, and the endless pot of fish chowder."

"And the totally transformed Mr. Wheeler," said Celia. "These heart stones are changing people and things. But how?"

"Maybe we should start by researching the stone," I suggested.

"Good idea," Celia said.

"But Celia, listen, I think we should keep this between us until we can figure out what's going on."

"Okay. Got it. Top Secret!" promised Celia.

As soon as we entered the library, we totally forgot about our English project. We went straight to the computer catalog to find books about stones. I typed GEOLOGY, STONES into the SEARCH box. Lots of book titles popped up: *Petrology—The Study of Stones, The Guide to Rocks and Minerals, Let's Rock, Granite & Gems.* We had started writing down the call numbers when we heard:

"Hi, Gale. Hi, Celia. Need any help finding something?" It was Mrs. Rosina, the librarian.

"Ahh, no, we're good. Maybe just point us in the direction of your geology books," I said.

"Homework?" she asked.

"Mmmm. Yup. Science class...we need to research this stone." Celia held out the heart stone.

So much for being Top Secret!

"Ahh—that's very familiar," said Mrs. Rosina. "Someone else in your class must be working on the same project."

"Same project?" I asked. "What do you mean?"

"Well, I found an identical stone here on Friday afternoon. One of your classmates must have left it behind," explained Mrs. Rosina. "Wait. Let me get it. I put it in the lost and found box."

I looked at Celia's shocked face and whispered, "Whoa! *Another* stone! This is crazy."

Mrs. Rosina returned and plopped the stone into my hand. "Maybe you can return it to your teacher? Now, which teacher is it?"

"Ahmmm...Miss Howard, Grade Four Science. Sure, I'll give it to her." I closed my fingers around the smooth stone. Energy vibrated through me.

"Great," said Mrs. Rosina. "Now, let's see. You'll find books about stones and gems in the science section. Aisle Five, bottom shelf on the right." She pointed to the far corner of the library.

"Thanks, Mrs. Rosina." We started to head toward the stacks of books, but my mind was racing...*Be a Detective...Ask questions*. I turned.

"Wait. Mrs. Rosina, where did you find this stone?"

"Here. In the library."

"No, I mean *where* in the library?" I asked.

"Oh, it was on a bookshelf...I believe it was in the travel section."

"*Where* in the travel section?"

"Hmmm...Why?"

"Well, I'm just asking because—because maybe my teacher can figure out which student left it behind."

"No problem. Follow me." Mrs. Rosina led us through the winding aisles of books.

"Now, let's see...I was returning books in this section." Mrs. Rosina squatted. "Right here. The stone was on this shelf."

"Are you sure?" I asked.

"Yes. This spot. I remember because I was putting back the Maine travel books."

"This spot—exactly?" I asked again.

Mrs. Rosina smiled and put her finger on the shelf. "Exactly."

"Thanks, Mrs. Rosina. Good to know," said Celia.

"Good luck on your project, girls." Mrs. Rosina headed back to the main desk, leaving us alone.

"There has to be a reason why that heart stone was placed here," said Celia.

I put the heart stone on the shelf on the exact spot Mrs. Rosina showed us. I jumped. "Did you see that?"

"See what?" asked Celia.

"The stone. It moved!"

"Try that again," instructed Celia.

I picked up the stone and gently put it back on the shelf. This time, the heart stone spun around until the tip of the heart pointed to books on the shelf.

"Wow!" said Celia. "This stone is trying to tell us something."

We looked at the books at the tip of the heart: *The Islands of Maine* and *Maine Coastal Currents and Tides*.

"Maybe these books will give us some clues," I said, gathering them into my arms. "Let's head to the science section."

We looked through some geology books with no luck, then found two giant stone and gem reference books. We hauled the books to the nearest table and settled in.

With the heart stones glistening in front of us, we both started looking through pages and pages of photographs to try to find a match.

"There's got to be a million stones here," said Celia.

"This could take all afternoon." I looked at the clock. It was three fifteen. "We're going to need a miracle."

Just as I spoke those words, I picked up one of the heart stones and rubbed it gently. Holding the stone in my fist, I closed my eyes. I felt a soothing energy, as if someone or something was guiding my hand. Still holding the stone, I let my pointer finger glide over the edges of the pages, until it abruptly stopped. I turned the page and opened my eyes.

"Here it is!"

Celia jumped out of her seat. We both stared at the image and then at the stones. The pink-reddish color matched perfectly.

"You found it!"

Together we read:

> RED QUARTZ—*Called the Love Stone or Heart Stone. Its color ranges from very light pink (almost white) to medium-dark red. Also known as Pink Quartz and Bohemian Ruby, this stone of universal love restores hope and harmony to family, friends, and community. Calming and reassuring, it brings feelings of peace, and comforts in times of grief. The presence of this lovely pink stone will not only send a soothing vibration to the person wearing it, but will resonate to those surrounding it. Known to have mystical powers, this stone absorbs energy and guides toward the truth.*

"That's amazing. It really *is* called a heart stone," said Celia.

We read the description again and again. Words popped out at us: *mystical powers...soothing vibration... guides toward the truth.*

I quickly took out my phone and snapped some pictures of the pages. Celia did the same. We returned the reference books to the shelf and made our way to the checkout desk with the two books we "found" in the travel section.

"So, was your research successful?" asked Mrs. Rosina.

Celia and I looked at each other. We could barely hide our excitement.

"Very successful! Thanks, Mrs. Rosina."

SIX

I made it to the LaundromArt in record time, dashing through the door at 4:01.

"A minute late," teased Emma as she handed me the stack of mail. "I did your pocket-emptying job. You can do the mail run."

"Did you find anything interesting in the deep dark world of pockets?" I joked.

"Don't know. I just put everything in the jar. Feel free to put on your gloves and search for treasures." Emma pushed the jar toward me and went back to her math homework.

I picked up the jar and jiggled it around. I peered inside: one silver button, three pennies, a shiny piece of sea glass, and a delicate lace flowered handkerchief. Thinking that the handkerchief might be something I should return, I reached in and pulled it out. Suddenly, plop, plop, plop…three pink heart stones tumbled out.

I gasped. "Emma, where did this handkerchief come from?"

"It came from one of those coats." Emma pointed toward the rack. Six coats hung side by side, ready for dry cleaning.

"Do you remember which coat?"

"Nope."

"You were supposed to put the stuff in envelopes and mark them!" I frantically pulled the coats off the rack, tossing them on the counter. "Was it this purple kid's coat or one of these adult coats? Was it this bright blue ski jacket or this long red wool coat? *Think*, Emma, *think*! This is important!"

"I wasn't paying much attention," confessed Emma.

"How can someone so smart not pay attention?"

"Because I only pay attention to important stuff, and the things people leave in their pockets are *not* important!" Emma was out of her seat, gathering her math book.

"They are to me!" I yelled. I held out the three heart stones. "These were wrapped in that handkerchief, and I need to figure out who they belong to!"

"Here we go again with the stupid stones," Emma said, her voice getting louder.

"They are *not* stupid!" I yelled, now nose to nose with Emma.

Just then, Mom and Captain rushed from the back.

"What's going on?" Captain asked.

"I can hear you girls screaming from my studio," said Mom.

"Emma emptied the pockets, and I found these heart stones wrapped in a handkerchief," I huffed. "She can't remember which coat they came from. I need to know."

Mom and Captain looked at the stones.

"Those stones sure are pretty," said Captain. "Can't say I ever saw stones quite like that around here."

"These are the 'magical' stones Gale is all gaga about!" said Emma.

"For your scientific information these are Red Quartz stones and they have mystical powers!" I blurted out.

"Ooh…mystical powers?" Emma hissed.

"Magic or no magic, these stones need to be returned to our customer," said Mom.

"That's if we can figure out *which* customer owns them!" I said.

"You're the detective!" Emma quipped.

"Both of you—enough. Emma, go do your homework in the back office. Gale, you *can* figure this out," said Mom. "Match the numbers on the coat tags to the numbers on the order forms. Then you'll have the customers' names and phone numbers. That will be a good place to start."

I located the small plastic tags on each coat and wrote down the six numbers. I looked through today's folder and pulled out the six matching order forms. One by one I scanned the last names: Appleton…Wong…Giorgio…DuPont…

I couldn't believe my eyes! *DuPont*! Phoebe DuPont—the wife of Pierre DuPont, the fisherman who was lost at sea.

"That has to be it!" I cheered.

"That has to be *what*?" asked Captain.

I wrapped Phoebe's red coat around me and brought a sleeve up to my nose. I breathed in, smelling the scent of salt air and seaweed. I put the three heart stones in the coat pocket. They settled in comfortably, like my fingers in my favorite mittens. I looked up at Captain. "I think Phoebe is the one who had a pocket full of heart stones."

"Well, I guess we can find out for sure on Wednesday. Come with me to deliver her coat. You can ask her yourself." Captain looked at his watch. "But right now, it's quarter to five. You'll never make it to the post office in time. I'll drive you. Meet me outside."

I put the three heart stones into my backpack, returned Phoebe's coat to the rack, and grabbed the mail.

"Captain will drop me home, Mom. See you later," I called.

Captain slowly backed the van out of the narrow driveway. He stopped and grinned through his untamed gray beard. "Get in, Windy."

Captain has nicknames for everyone. I'm Windy and Emma is Einstein. Captain's nickname is Captain. His real name is Russell Jackson, but no one ever calls him Russell. The only reason I know his real name is because I snooped at his pay stub. For years Captain was the skipper of the Cliff Cove ferry. He shuttled people to and from the surrounding islands seven days a week. Now that he's retired, the only thing he shuttles is laundry.

"Those stones seem pretty important to you. Why do you think they belong to Phoebe DuPont?" Captain asked.

Captain's question jolted me. I looked at his kind face. Since his wife died and his kids moved away, Emma and I have become his "stand-in grandkids." Through the years, Captain was always there to help me figure things out, whether it was a math problem, a broken chain on my bike, or how to deal with missing my friend Kayla. Maybe he could help me figure this out too.

"Well, Captain, there is more to the story. I've been finding heart stones around town. On Friday, I found two heart stones at the fisherman statue, right near the flowers from the vigil. There has to be a connection."

"Really? The fisherman statue. Okay, then. Phoebe might be able to give you some help."

"Thanks, Captain," I said.

"I'm glad we're dropping by Phoebe's. I was planning on visiting her myself anyway, check on her, see how she's doing." Captain shook his head. "I still can't believe

Pierre is gone. Boy, do I miss him." Captain's voice trailed off. He was quiet for a bit, then looked at me with a smile that wrinkled his whole face.

"But you know, Windy, we have to focus on the happy times, and making deliveries with you will be like the good ol' days. Remember how much fun we had?"

"Sure. It was great," I said.

I lied. Last August I *thought* that making deliveries with Captain might be fun. I envisioned a few quick deliveries and then an afternoon lounging at the beach. No such luck. I discovered that Captain was a "talker," and he knew everyone in town. One time I ended up being trapped for two hours sitting with blue-haired old ladies in Bea's Beauty Shop while Captain volunteered to try to fix the clogged sink. Another time, the typical speedy linen drop-off at Milly's Cafe turned into a long, card-playing, town gossipy coffee break when Captain spotted Pierre at "their" corner table. The only good thing about that delivery was Milly's potato donuts. This delivery would be different. This time I would be the one doing the talking and hopefully getting some answers.

We made it to the post office just in time. I mailed some letters and picked up a package. Captain dropped me at home before Mom and Emma got there.

The first thing I did was text Celia.

GH—You are not going to believe this! I found three heart stones at the LaundromArt. I think they came from Phoebe DuPont's pocket.

CS—What? Three? Wow! So, you really think they are Phoebe's?

GH—It's just a hunch, but it makes sense. I'll find out on Wednesday after school. I'm going with Captain to deliver the coat to Phoebe. Do you want to come?

CS—You know I do!

GH—Awesome. I'll tell Captain. He loves company.

CS— Oh, wait. Wednesday. Can't. Piano lessons...Okay, that's it. I'm ditching piano. This is way too important. Count me in.

GH—All right. Plan on going to the LaundromArt with me right after school on Wednesday.

CS—Got it. And I'm going to talk to my sister again. Maybe I can find out if Angela remembers seeing Phoebe in the diner.

GH—Good plan. See you at school tomorrow.

I tossed the phone on my bed and took a new note-book from my top shelf. Detectives needed to keep good notes and carry a real notebook everywhere. There was no way I'd type this stuff in my phone or my school computer. It was time to write everything down. I lined up the heart stones on my desk, opened the notebook, and wrote:

Eight heart stones Celia—1, Sam—1, Gale (me)—6

TIMELINE: ♥

FRIDAY-2:45pm   1 stone found by Sam / guitar case
FRIDAY-afterschool   1 stone found by Mrs. Rosina / library
FRIDAY-4:15pm   2 stones found by Me / Fisherman Statue
SATURDAY-Time?   1 stone found by Angela (Celia's sister) / Dolphin Diner
MONDAY-4:10pm   3 stones found in LaundromArt / coat pocket / Phoebe DuPont??

I grabbed my phone and uploaded the photos I'd taken from the gemstone book, printed them, and glued them on the next few notebook pages. I wrote CLUES across the top and highlighted the description of Red Quartz.

Just then, Mom knocked on my bedroom door, then poked her head in. "Dinner will be ready in five."

"Okay, Mom." I looked at my timeline. "Hey, Mom, when did Phoebe drop off her coat?"

"Hmmm. She came in on Friday afternoon."

"What time? I didn't see her."

"About four o'clock. I think you were on the way to the post office."

"That's it!" I cheered.

"What's *it*?"

I tapped my pen on my notebook. "Phoebe was downtown on Friday afternoon. She has to be the one putting the heart stones all around town: Sam's guitar case, the library, the fisherman statue…her coat."

"Wait," said Mom. "You didn't tell me you found more heart stones." Mom looked at the stones on my desk. "Six?"

"Actually, eight. Celia has one from the Dolphin Diner. Her sister Angela found it in the tip jar. And Sam has one." I paused, twirling one of the stones with my finger. "I didn't tell you because you and Emma and even Dad think I'm some kind of wacky person, imagining things."

"Gale, seems to me that they're just very pretty stones that need to be returned. Mystery solved."

"Not really, Mom. I need to know *why* they are showing up around town and—"

"Well, if they *are* Phoebe's stones," Mom interrupted, "I'm sure she'll have an explanation. Maybe it's some kind of conceptual creative project. She's an artist, you know. Or maybe, just maybe, she has a hole in her pocket!" Mom chuckled. "Come on, let's eat. Everything is probably burnt to a crisp."

Before I closed my notebook, I updated my notes:

FRIDAY-4:00pm　　Phoebe DuPont drops off coat
　　　　　　　　　(with three heart stones wrapped in
　　　　　　　　　a handkerchief)

I looked at the heart stones. Mom was wrong. These stones were more than just stones. There was a bigger mystery here that I didn't dare bring up to my mom... the magical part. She probably wouldn't believe me anyway. These stones were changing things and changing people. It was almost like the stones were leaving clues, sending messages, but why? Hopefully, Phoebe could help me figure all this out. I looked at my calendar and groaned. Her answers were two days away. There's one thing I wasn't good at, and that was waiting.

SEVEN

Tuesday crawled by. It was the longest school day ever. I wanted to talk to Celia in private, but we always seemed to be surrounded by a million kids. Finally, at the end of the day, Celia found me at my locker.

"Any news from your sister?" I asked.

"I talked to her last night and asked her if Phoebe ate at the diner recently."

"Well...?"

"Angela said Phoebe came in for lunch on Friday, about one o'clock. Angela was actually pretty shocked to see her. The last time she saw Phoebe was in August, when her husband, Pierre, and Mr. Wheeler had some heated words. I guess Pierre was pretty upset that he wasn't supporting local fishermen. Anyway, Angela was her waitress on Friday. And guess what she ordered?"

"Fish chowder?"

"You got it."

"Wait. The timing doesn't fit. Didn't your sister find the heart stone on Saturday?"

"Exactly! Do you want to know why? They didn't count Friday's tip jar until Saturday morning!"

"*Yes*! If Phoebe dropped the heart stone in the tip jar on Friday, that means that *all* eight stones were scattered around town on Friday afternoon between one and four." I high-fived Celia. "That's awesome detective work!"

"We rock!" Celia smiled, poking me with her elbow. "Get it?—rock—stone? Maybe we should call ourselves the Rockettes?"

Celia looked at my confused face.

"Rockettes? The famous New York City dancers? I went to their Broadway Christmas show last year."

I didn't know them, but of course Celia did. She started kicking her long legs. I joined her. We linked arms and danced ourselves down the hall, laughing the whole way. Celia danced herself right out the door, while I made my way to the gym for the first day of soccer practice. Everyone whined about being in the smelly gym on a sunny day, but the field was still a mud bowl. While I was at soccer practice, Emma was at the Robotics Team meeting.

After our activities ended at four o'clock, I met up with Emma, and we went straight home. We let ourselves in and headed to the kitchen, where Mom had left us instructions to start dinner. Our kitchen was tiny, but it had a huge personality with its orange-painted cabinets and teal countertops. Mom's collection of 1960s posters lined the wall, while a vintage white-and-yellow daisy light fixture hung over the table.

I quickly popped the tray of lasagna into the oven, put the sauce on the stove to simmer, and set the table. I was anxious to get going on my detective work. By the time Emma had finished making the salad, I was already settled in the big comfy chair in the living room, surrounded by my research.

"Well, you definitely live up to your name," said Emma. "It looks like gale-force winds blew through here!"

"Don't move any of my papers. You'll mess them up."

"You can't mess up a mess."

"Believe it or not, I know exactly where everything is."

"Not."

I watched as Emma slowly emptied her backpack. She neatly stacked her books on the coffee table, forming a precise pyramid. Then she slowly lined up her yellow pencils. Just watching her drove me crazy. I refocused on my own work, updating my Top Secret notebook:

FRIDAY-1pm   Dolphin Diner (Phoebe adds one stone
                 to Tip Jar?)

I grabbed my library books, opening *The Islands of Maine*. It was time to figure out the heart stone connection. I unfolded the map that came along with the book.

"Whoa. Did you know there are three thousand one hundred sixty-six islands off the coast of Maine?"

Emma's ears perked up. "Yup...and a lot of those islands are tiny, more like big rocks. Some are less than a half mile wide. They call them islets."

For a sixth grader, my sister was pretty smart. I started reading. "Listen to some of these island names. I bet you've never heard of these...Bald Porcupine, Black Duck, No Mans, Pirate Island...and there are even Seven Sisters Islands."

"Yup. I know."

Figures. Emma knew everything. She picked up the *Currents and Tides* book. "Good reference book. I used that for my tide project. What's your homework?" she asked.

"Not homework. It's just research."

"Non-school research? Don't tell me...heart stones?" Emma turned to me. "Gale, you need strong evidence to get to the facts. What do you have?"

"Umm...I think that..."

"See—you *think*. Not good enough. You just have a bunch of hunches."

"Well, I have proof."

"Proof?"

"Wait here." I ran to my room.

"Here. Look at this." I gave Emma the card. "Friday, on my way to the post office, I found two heart stones at the base of the statue, right next to fresh roses and this card. Our card! Remember? We saw it Friday after school. Look at it now!"

Emma examined the front of the card, and then opened it. "Impossible! This card was totally drenched. Now you're trying to trick me. Did you just make this?"

"No! Really, it was there, and fresh flowers too… exactly like the bouquet we left in February. Red roses with a big yellow bow!"

"Yeah, right! So you're telling me that our card reappeared all dry and perfect and that fresh flowers arrived out of nowhere? That's nuts. If you're not playing a trick on me, then someone is playing a trick on you!"

I sank heavily into the chair and closed my eyes. "I give up," I said under my breath.

"That's good, Gale. You should give up this crazy idea!"

After that, I didn't say a word. I shouldn't have shown her anything. I wanted to scream, "I'm giving up on *you!*" but I didn't. I was done talking to her. What was the use? There was no way I would ever convince her.

EIGHT

The next morning, I woke up early. Finally, Wednesday, the day we would get to talk to Phoebe. Before I even got dressed, I carefully gathered all the heart stones, gently put them in an orange woolen sock, and stuffed it in the bottom of my backpack. At breakfast, I gave Emma the silent treatment. I wasn't going to let her constant nay-saying ruin my day. She shrugged and buried her nose in her science book. Good.

At school, I couldn't concentrate. I sat in English class watching the sunlight cast dancing shadows on my desk. Mr. Elliot was saying something, but it sounded like he was talking from underwater...all I heard was blub-blub-blub. When he looked my way, I pretended to take notes, but what I was really doing was writing a list of questions to ask Phoebe. The day dragged on. Finally, the school bell rang and it was time—time to get some answers.

"Hey, wait up! What's the hurry?" Emma called as she ran to catch up.

I looked at Celia. "Please tell Emma that we're going on deliveries with Captain so we can talk to Phoebe. He's waiting for us."

Celia echoed my message to Emma.

"Oh. Right. You're still not talking to me." Emma looked at Celia. "Tell Gale, good luck with flakey Phoebe DuPont."

I walked along pretending I wasn't listening.

"That woman is a little weird," Emma continued. "That's it! That's your answer! Why didn't I think of it before? Phoebe is the one pulling these pranks! It's just an outrageous hoax!"

"Wait. You know her?" Celia asked.

"She lives on Hollow Point, right? I don't *really* know her but I met her once, in September. Our science group was charting the tides and currents and we ended up on the cove right in front of her house. I'll never forget it. We were walking along the beach and we saw this woman with a long flowing skirt and flowers in her hair, dancing by herself on the beach. Our teacher, Mr. Caruso, knows her so he stopped to chat and before you knew it, the whole group was up on her deck drinking this disgusting arugula iced tea. It tasted worse than dirty turtle water."

I looked at Celia and made a disgusting face. I wanted to know how Emma knew what dirty turtle water tasted like, but I wasn't about to ask her.

"So we were sitting there on her deck, surrounded by about ten sea glass wind chimes, all making a racket, when she pointed to her side yard. It was filled with strange, gigantic driftwood and seaweed sculptures. She told us how the sea *calls* her and she went on and on about how she creates these one-of-a-kind sculptures out of the natural beauty the sea sends to her shore. Looking at them, I couldn't help but think that with one match we could make an awesome bonfire. Then there were the stacks of rocks…"

"Rocks? What rocks?" Celia asked.

"They call them cairns; they're handmade small towers of rocks. She said she builds them to honor Mother Nature. They were all over the cove."

"I've seen cairns before. They're not easy to build. I tried," said Celia.

"Right…it's all about gravity and balance," explained Emma. "Anyway, finally Mr. Caruso made up some ridiculous excuse and we quickly escaped to the beach. All I can say is, *be ready*! I'll bet you a thousand bucks that you're going to find out that your magical heart stone mystery is a big giant lie and that Phoebe is one crazy lady!"

Celia and I looked at each other and shrugged. I gave her a big thumbs-up, grabbed Celia's arm, kicked my legs, and danced on the sidewalk. Finally, I broke my silence.

"The Rockettes are ready!"

"You guys are so lame," said Emma. "Don't say I didn't warn you!" With that, Emma made a quick beeline to the other side of the street.

I watched her walk along, looking straight ahead with her nose up in the air. The distance between us was only twenty feet, but it felt like we were miles apart.

"I can't believe you are sisters; you're nothing alike. You don't even look alike," said Celia.

"I know. Sometimes I can't believe it either," I said. "Sometimes I feel like I don't even belong in my own family."

"You'll see, Gale," said Celia. "Once everyone knows the whole story, they'll come around."

That made me think. Mom and Dad didn't actually know the whole story. So far, I had only told them bits and pieces. But this mystery was far from solved. It was best to keep them in the dark about the magical part, for now.

"You know what we need?" I said. "We need more proof!"

"And today we are going to get it!" said Celia.

As soon as we turned the corner, we saw Captain in the driveway loading up the van.

"Good timing, Windy." Captain opened up the back van door, took off his baseball hat, and bowed. "Welcome, ladies."

"Hi, Captain. This my friend Celia, Celia Shen."

"A pleasure to meet you, Celia. I heard a lot about you."

"Thanks for letting me tag along," said Celia as she hopped in.

I threw my backpack on the seat. It landed with a thump, startling Celia. I winked. "Heart stones—they're heavy!" I turned to Captain. "Be right back. I just want to say hi to Mom."

"Okay. Hey, grab that last box of linens by the door," said Captain.

"Got it."

I ran through the side door directly into Mom's studio. The place looked like a rainbow exploded. Colorful wood block prints were hanging from one end of the studio to the other. Mom emerged from the sea of color.

"Printing day!"

"I can tell!" I laughed. "Love the look." Mom's dark hair was pulled back in a big messy bun, and her shirt was covered with splatters of color. Somehow Mom managed to get paint on her face. Smudges of purple and blue smeared her olive skin.

"Everyone says we look alike, and now I see it…casual but colorful!" I teased.

"Roman nose and all," Mom said, smiling, playfully dotting my nose with yellow paint.

I wiped the paint off with the back of my hand and grabbed the box of linens. "Just letting you know we're leaving now, heading out on deliveries," I said.

"Good luck with Phoebe. I want to know what she says."

I paused. Mmmm. She wanted to know what Phoebe said? That was good.

"I will. And I've been thinking. You know how you always tell me to follow my inner voice?"

"That's right."

"That's what I'm doing." I gave my mom a kiss on the cheek, the purple one. "See you later." I hoisted the box on my hip. "Oh, and by the way, I like my nose!"

NINE

I climbed in the backseat of the van and buckled up.

"Okay, we're off," announced Captain. "Windy, I need to make a few quick stops on the way to Hollow Point. Won't take long. I know you girls are anxious to get there."

Anxious. That's for sure. I had a pit in my stomach. I looked at Celia. She was nibbling on her fingernails.

A half mile down the road, Captain pulled over. "First stop. Be right back." We watched Captain lug a big stack of white towels into Main Street Barbershop.

Emma's words were circling in my head...*Phoebe...crazy lady...big lie...outrageous hoax.*

"Can't be," I said out loud.

"What can't be?"

"What Emma said—there's no way this heart stone mystery is a hoax. No one could make all these things happen. I hope Phoebe can give us some answers."

"And if she doesn't?" asked Celia.

"Then we go to Plan B."

"Do we have a Plan B?"

"Plan B is to come up with a Plan B!"

We high-fived. What a team!

Captain jumped back in the van, and we drove out of downtown on the long narrow causeway, which was surrounded by water on both sides. The tiny houses looked like they were holding onto the land for dear life. I think they were. During the storm, many houses lost their grip and slipped into the sea. Just past the row of houses, beyond the causeway, was Kayla's house. Several pickup trucks were parked on the edge of the road. Ladders and workers surrounded the bright blue house, which was dotted with boarded-up windows. The side door was nailed shut with a giant wooden X marking the spot where the hungry sea gobbled up the deck. It didn't look like Kayla would be returning to Cliff Cove anytime soon.

Within minutes, we were on a tree-lined peninsula and traveling on Atlantic Way, a long bumpy dirt road leading to Hollow Point. Captain stopped at two more places, first dropping a box of linens at Salty's Restaurant and then a quick stop at Doc Jay's fancy Victorian house on the hill. The road curved to the right as we approached Hollow Point.

"Look!" I pointed out the window at a mailbox perched on a driftwood base. Faded hand-painted letters spelled out P & P DuPont. I reached out and squeezed Celia's hand.

"This is it!"

Captain pulled the van onto the gravel driveway and parked next to the small gray weathered house. Celia and I hopped out of the van and were jolted by the cold breeze blowing off the cove. We both zipped up our coats.

Captain looked toward the shore. "There's Phoebe. You two go on down and say hi. I'm going to organize this stuff and pull out her coat."

We slowly walked toward the beach, fighting against the wind. Cairns of all sizes surrounded the cove. Phoebe spotted us from a distance and waved. We watched her take a few steps, stop, bend over, dig a little, then walk a bit more. When we got closer, we were greeted by her smiling rosy face, which was framed by a multi-colored knit hat. Her long grayish-white braid cascaded down her back.

"Hello, girls. I'm Phoebe. Captain said he might have some helpers."

Celia reached out her hand. "I'm Celia."

"And I'm Gale. Well, we're not really helpers. We actually came because we wanted to return some things that may belong to you."

"Oh really? What did I leave behind now?"

Just then, I realized I had left the heart stones in the van. "Ahh, well…a small, flowered handkerchief and… mmmm, some stones, like pinkish-red stones, shaped like…"

"Hearts? Stones like this?" Phoebe opened her hand. In it was a single red glistening heart stone.

"Yes! Just like that!" Celia said, surprised.

"I found this one just now." Suddenly, Phoebe put the stone to her lips, kissed it, and closed her eyes. "I love you too, Pierre," she said softly.

I looked at Celia, then at Phoebe. After an awkward moment, Phoebe's eyes opened. "Ahh, yes. The stones."

"They're yours then? The heart stones?" I asked.

"They could be. Girls, let's go inside."

We all walked to the van, where Captain was standing holding Phoebe's long red wool coat wrapped in thin plastic. I grabbed my backpack from the backseat, and we followed Phoebe into her house.

"Nice to see you, Captain," said Phoebe as she opened the bright yellow door.

"How are you doing, Phoebe?" asked Captain.

"It hasn't been easy, but life does not always go as we plan." Phoebe took the coat from Captain and hung it in the small hall closet, then rummaged through her purse and handed Captain a rolled-up bill. "Thank you."

Captain stepped back, waving his hand. "Please. No tip. Really."

Phoebe stuffed the bill in his pocket. "Now, Captain, you work hard!"

Captain gave up. "Okay, okay. But next time you come into town, I'm treating you to one of Milly's potato donuts!"

"That would be delightful. And we'll sit at Pierre's table and have his favorite, Sea Salt Maple, in his honor." Phoebe tried to smile through her sadness, then gestured toward the kitchen. "Everyone, please come in. Take a seat."

We took off our boots in the hall and hung our coats on the hooks. Phoebe ushered us to the table. "How about some nice hot tea?"

I looked at Celia with raised eyebrows remembering Emma's story. I guess we might just find out what dirty turtle water tastes like after all.

"Tea all around," said Captain as we settled in our chairs.

My eyes explored the tiny house. It was stuffed to the brim with antique furniture, artwork, seashells, globes, nautical maps, and plants…lots of plants. The windowsill by the table was crowded with travel souvenirs, photographs, and *more* plants, all leaning toward the window, fighting for the sunlight. Then I saw it. I nudged Celia with my elbow and pointed. A huge glass jar filled with pinkish-red heart stones stood in the corner of the sill. With a *clink*, Phoebe added one more.

Phoebe arranged cookies on a plate and poured us each a cup of tea. It didn't smell too bad. I took a sip and added lots of sugar. Celia did the same. Captain drank his straight up.

"So, the heart stones...you found some?" Phoebe scooted her chair up to the table.

"Yes, we did." I moved my cup to the side, opened up my backpack, and gently spread out the flowered hand-kerchief on the table. I reached into my backpack again, pulled out the woolen sock and emptied the heart stones onto the handkerchief. Celia pried her heart stone out of her jean pocket and added it to the pile.

"I found three heart stones wrapped in this hand-kerchief in a coat pocket at the LaundromArt. The other stones are from around town. Are they yours?" I asked.

"That's my handkerchief. Isn't it gorgeous? I got that in Venice five years ago. Handmade lace..."

I was getting impatient. Not for nothing, but we really didn't care about the handkerchief. "What about the heart stones?" I asked.

"The stones? Hmmm...Yes, they are mine, too." Phoebe motioned to the huge jar. "You mentioned you found three in a coat pocket? I assume my coat pocket? Where did you find the others?"

"Don't *you* know?" I thought that was a very odd question.

"Refresh my memory," said Phoebe.

I rattled off all the locations: a guitar case on Main Street, the fisherman statue, the Dolphin Diner, and the library.

"Oh, dear. All those places?"

"I don't understand," said Celia. "You said they were your stones. Did someone else scatter the heart stones around town?"

Phoebe put her hands on her face, briefly closed her eyes, and took a long deep breath.

"No. It was me. I did go to town to scatter the heart stones. I just don't remember everything clearly." She paused, reached over, and picked up a stone.

"Let me back up. It all began a few days after the Valentine's Day storm. I was feeling particularly low, you know, missing my Pierre. I looked out this very window and the sun was shining so bright that the water sparkled like gold. I felt like the cove was calling me. It was a frigid day, so I bundled up and took a little walk down to the shore. As I always do, I look at the ground when I walk. I'm always searching for treasures. Suddenly, I saw a stone poking out of the sand. It had a very unusual color, one that I had never seen before, like a reddish-pink. I squatted down, took off my glove, and whittled it out of the sand. When I wiped it clean, I saw right away that it was a beautiful stone in the shape of a perfect heart. I tell you, I cried right then and there. There was no doubt that the heart-shaped stone was from my Pierre. He was sending me his love. I kissed the stone and said, 'I love you too, Pierre.'"

Celia and I and even Captain were staring at Phoebe, hanging onto every word.

"Since that day, I have walked the beach daily, no matter what the weather, and every day I find one, two, and sometimes three heart stones. I think I've collected over fifty stones. To me, they are signs from heaven. This jar is filled with love. Last week, I had this unshakable urge to grab a pocketful of heart stones and go into town. I was thinking, my dear Pierre wants me to spread some love."

"What day? Was it Friday?" I asked.

"As a matter of fact, it *was* Friday. I know that for sure because Friday was my dear Pierre's birthday."

It was all starting to fit together.

"When I got to town, I parked in the center and just began walking. I had no particular plan. I remember passing a young man with a guitar. Pierre just loved music."

I eyed Celia. "Sam found a heart stone in his case," I said.

"Really?" Phoebe continued, "My stomach rumbled just as I approached the Dolphin Diner. Now the crazy thing is, Pierre and Mr. Wheeler never got along. Pierre didn't like the fact that Mr. Wheeler bought his fish in Portland instead of buying the fish fresh here, in Cliff

Cove, from the locals. Sorry, I digress. So anyway, something just pulled me into the diner and before I knew it, I was sitting at a table, ordering fish chowder, which was very good, by the way. You say you found a heart stone there?"

"Yes," said Celia. "My sister did. In the tip jar. She was your waitress."

"Do you remember adding a stone to the tip jar?" I asked.

"Vaguely. That entire day was a blur. It was like my body was walking through a sea of mud. I can't quite remember where I went after the diner."

"The fisherman statue? The library?" I was trying to jog her memory.

"Mmmm. Well, I always go to the fisherman statue when I'm in town to say a little prayer for Pierre and Carlos. So, I suspect I was there. The library? Oh! I think I was there!" She reached over to the counter and handed me a book. "I was wondering where this came from."

I looked at the book's cover: *Trumpet Sounds* by Miles Cassidy. I tapped Celia's arm and pointed to the due date sticker. Two weeks from Friday. Proof.

"Now, I *do* remember going to the LaundromArt. After walking around in my bulky sweater and big coat, I was feeling rather warm, so I thought—might as well get my winter coat dry-cleaned. I chatted with the owner, Anna. I met her at the Art Association meeting last fall. Lovely lady."

"That's my mom."

"Ahh—I should have realized. You look just like her. You have the same beautiful big brown eyes. Anyway, from there, I drove home."

"How many heart stones did you have in your pockets before you headed into town?" I asked.

"Oh goodness, two handfuls? Maybe eight or ten stones."

I picked up the jar. "Phoebe, reach in and take out two handfuls."

Phoebe cooperated and pulled out a bunch of stones and placed them on the table. We counted. Eleven.

Celia and I looked at each other and nodded. We knew eight heart stones had been found. There could be a few more we hadn't found yet.

"Phoebe, do you remember going anywhere else?" I asked.

"My, you girls are quite inquisitive. I may have, but like I said, the day was a blur until I got to the LaundromArt."

"So, do you think these heart stones are leaving messages?" Celia got right to the point.

"Messages? Hmmm. Well, I think, as I mentioned, Pierre is sending me his love and watching over me from above. The heart stones give me a sense of peace. Maybe he lured me to town because he just wanted everyone to know that he is okay up there in heaven."

"We think there is more to it," I said.

"More?" said Captain and Phoebe together. Captain had been quietly taking in the whole thing. I had told him about finding the stones, but I hadn't told him about any of the unusual details. He helped himself to a second cup of tea and leaned back in his chair, like he was planning on staying a while.

"Well, Phoebe…and Captain, we think the heart stones have some kind of magic powers. They seem to be giving people hope, changing things, leaving clues."

"Changing things? Leaving clues? Like what?" asked Phoebe.

"And why?" added Captain.

"We haven't figured that out yet. But there was the fish chowder situation," Celia began.

"Situation?" asked Captain, leaning forward on the table.

"The soup pot at Dolphin Diner just kept producing a never-ending supply of fish chowder. And Mr. Wheeler… he gave it all away!" explained Celia.

"Now that *is* a miracle!" joked Captain.

Phoebe started laughing hysterically. "Mr. Wheeler? I can't imagine Mr. Wheeler giving anything away. That would be just like Pierre to make that happen."

"And then I found two more at the fisherman statue," I continued. All the heart stone stories just poured out…the transformed cards and flowers, Sam's new talent, the spinning stone at the library. This time it was Phoebe and Captain who were hanging onto every word.

"Well, I'll be. There may be something to these heart stones after all," said Captain.

"Girls, I don't know where this is going, but what I do know is that the heart stones keep washing up on shore and I'm going to keep collecting them and listening to my heart. And wherever the energy of the heart stones moves me, I will follow."

"We will follow them too, Phoebe. Thank you," I said.

Phoebe scribbled her phone number on a piece of paper, and we did the same. We all agreed to keep in touch. We were just about to leave when Phoebe handed me the sock full of heart stones.

"Girls, please, keep these heart stones. The heart stones will lead you. Follow your heart and keep your minds open. Spread the love. Pierre would like that."

"We will."

The three of us crowded in the tiny hall and slipped into our boots and coats. We listened as Phoebe started humming, then singing a beautiful song. I was glad the heart stones brought her some peace.

When we got into the van, there was a moment of shocked silence. Our minds were spinning trying to make sense of it all.

"Well, this went way better than I thought it would," I finally said, grasping the lumpy woolen sock on my lap. "We found out that the heart stones are washing up on Hollow Point and we know for sure that Phoebe is the one leaving the heart stones around town."

"But now we have a bigger mystery," said Celia. "Where are all these stones coming from?"

"Phoebe seems to be convinced that Pierre is sending them…from heaven." I had a hard time even saying the words.

"But really? How can it be Pierre? No one is ever going to believe us now," Celia said.

"Okay, girls," Captain piped in from the front seat. "I'm not one for believing in the supernatural, but after listening to Phoebe and all the things you girls said, I'm becoming a believer. All this is a little crazy, but it's almost too strange to make up. You girls sure do have a case to solve."

I hugged the woolen sock and looked at Celia.

"What's the next step?" she asked.

I took one heart stone out of the sock and gave it to Celia. "One of these is yours. Keep it with you. Like Phoebe told us, the heart stones will lead. We have to follow our hearts and keep our minds open."

TEN

After Captain dropped Celia at her house, we drove to the LaundromArt and pulled into the driveway just as Mom and Emma were locking up the place.

"How did it go?" asked Mom.

"Good, I..."

My thoughts were interrupted by music. Familiar music. My eyes followed the sound.

"I think Sam only knows one song," said Emma.

"I heard this song before," I said.

"Hellllo? That's because Sam has been singing the same song since Friday," teased Emma. "What kind of detective are you anyway?"

I ignored Emma and turned toward Sam, giving the song my full attention.

The Tide of Love
> *Brings you back to me*
Follow your heart into the sea

"Wait a minute!" I looked at Captain. "That's the same song Phoebe was singing!" I ran to the corner. Captain followed.

Strong like the ocean
> *A moonbeam away*
Our love is closer day by day

The heavens are watching
> *From clouds above*
No one can stop
> *The Tide of Love*

The Tide of Love
> *Brings you back to me*
Follow your heart into the sea

When Sam finished the last note, I got his attention. "Awesome, Sam. Where's that song from?" I asked.

"Man—it was crazy! These lyrics and the tune just popped into my head! Right out of the blue."

"What? When?"

"Friday. Right after I saw you."

"The day you found the heart stone?" *My* heart was pounding.

"Yup," said Sam. "You were right, Gale. The stone is special. I keep it with me all the time." He patted his vest pocket.

"Are you saying you never heard that song before?" I asked.

"Nope. Like I said. It just came to me."

"Can you sing it again?"

This time I took out my cell phone and pressed RECORD. I looked at Captain. I could tell he was as shocked as I was.

> *The Tide of Love*
> > *Brings you back to me*
> *Follow your heart into the sea*

After the song ended, I blurted out, "*Follow your heart into the sea.* It's a clue!"

"I think you're right, Windy," said Captain.

"Right about what? What are you talking about?" Mom and Emma were now standing behind us.

"Mom, Phoebe was singing that same song today."

"Okay? Now, why is that a big deal?" asked Mom. "I must be missing something."

"It's the heart stones. They're leaving clues." I looked at my mom's confused expression. "Mom, I have a lot I need to tell you."

"Be ready, Mom. She'll fill your head with story-scams," said Emma.

Suddenly, I lost it. "Emma, can you please open your mind for once in your life? Maybe you don't know everything! Maybe there *is* such a thing as magic." I could feel my face getting hot.

"Calm down, Gale, before you explode," said Emma. "I think the rocks went to your head!"

"Okay, girls, enough. I'm exhausted. Let's go home," said Mom.

I turned to Captain. "Thanks, Captain."

"Sure thing, Windy. Now, tell your mom *everything*. Everything that Phoebe told you and everything that you told Phoebe. I'm ready to help." Captain winked. "Good detective work." He tipped his hat toward my mom, crossed the street, and got into his rusty black truck.

"Now I'm very intrigued," said Mom.

As we walked home, Sam's music slowly faded.

"So, what was that all about?" asked Mom.

I glanced at Emma; she was walking right in front of us, with her hood up. "Can we talk later, Mom?" I whispered.

Mom nodded and patted my back. "Sure thing."

My mind was spinning. I was trying to piece these clues together and figure it all out. The only thing I knew for certain was that I had to talk to Mom in private, without Emma. But first, I had something important to do.

As soon as I got in the door, I went directly into my bedroom and uploaded the song onto my computer. I put on headphones and listened to the song again, not once, not twice, but five times, writing the lyrics in my detective notebook. I then rummaged through my backpack until I found the crumpled piece of paper. I looked at Phoebe's phone number, held my breath, and dialed. The phone rang and rang. I was just about to hang up when I heard:

"Hello?"

"Hi, Phoebe. It's Gale. Umm. We met today…"

"Of course. It was such a pleasure to meet you, Gale. Did you forget something?"

"No. It's just—I have another question."

"Sure, dear. What is it?"

"When we were leaving, you were singing a song. It went like this…" I sang the first line. "*The Tide of Love…*"

"Oh, yes." I heard Phoebe sigh.

"The song? Where did you learn it?" I asked.

"Learn it? I've lived with it for years. It's an old song from Pierre's family, passed down through the generations. His father sang the song in French to Pierre when he was a small boy. Pierre grew up in Nova Scotia, you know, a family of fishermen. Anyway, Pierre's father sang that song to him before going off to sea and Pierre sang that same song to me before he left on his many fishing trips. It is such a lovely song. It keeps me close to Pierre."

Phoebe started singing. I listened as she sang the entire song, her voice cracking. Then there was a sad silence. I could tell she was crying. "Isn't it beautiful?" she said.

"Yes, it is." I had a lump in my throat.

"Gale. Is there anything else?"

"Umm. No. That was it, Phoebe. It's such a great song. I just wanted to know more about it."

"Well, aren't you sweet? Let's stay in touch, dear."

"We will. Thanks, Phoebe."

As soon as I hung up, I texted Celia.

☺

GH— Celia, remember that song Phoebe was singing as we were heading out the door?

CS—Maybe. Sort of. Why?

GH— Sam was singing it.

CS— I'm confused.

GH— I need to call you to explain. Is now a good time?

CS— YUP.

☺

Unlike Phoebe, Celia answered on the first ring.

Just then Mom poked her head into my room. "Dinner's ready."

"Hold on, Celia."

I looked at Mom and pointed to the phone. "Start without me." I was starving, but this call was way more important than reheated leftovers.

"Sorry, Celia. I'm back."

"Okay. The song? What about it?"

"Well, I just heard Sam sing the same exact song that Phoebe was singing," I said.

"So, maybe it's a popular song?" said Celia.

"Sam said that the song just 'popped in his head.' He said he had never heard it before. Listen to this."

I put my cell phone up to my computer and played the entire song.

"Celia. It's a clue! I called Phoebe. She said it was an old family song, and Pierre sang it to her every time he headed out to sea to go fishing. The crazy thing is this song 'popped' into Sam's head on *Friday*, right after he found the heart stone. He's been singing it ever since and is convinced that he created it."

"Gale, you're talking way too fast. What exactly is the clue?"

I repeated the last lines of the song slowly:

"*The Tide of Love*
    Brings you back to me
Follow your heart into the sea."

"We have to follow the heart stones. *Brings you back to me*...I think Pierre is talking through Sam. I think Pierre wants us to go into the sea."

"Us? What? Go into the sea? How?"

"Captain," I said. "No one knows the coastal waters better than him. He was the captain of the island ferry for over thirty years."

"Will he help us?" asked Celia.

"I think he will."

"Now we just have to figure out where the heck to look. The ocean is huge."

"Celia, remember what Phoebe said? *The heart stones will lead you. Follow your heart and keep your minds open.*"

"Okay. Mind open."

"These heart stones have powers. I'm sure of it. I'll talk to Captain. See you tomorrow at school."

We hung up. "School," I mumbled. It had been five days since the first heart stones were discovered and during those five days, I had done zero homework. I gathered my math folder and tried to get through three fraction worksheets. Forty minutes later my stomach won over the equations. I walked into the kitchen. It was empty and dark. The daisy light over the table glowed, illuminating a foil-covered plate. My dinner. I took off the foil and popped the plate of broccoli and pasta into the microwave. I heard music coming from Emma's room. Now was a good time for me to finally talk to Mom. I followed the soft murmur of the television into the living room. Mom was fast asleep on the couch, an open book on her lap. My talk with Mom would have to wait.

ELEVEN

The next morning, I was running late. The heart stone mystery was stealing my sleep and hijacking my school life. I was hoping to talk to Mom at breakfast, but Emma was at the kitchen table, digging into a syrup-drenched waffle, while hiding behind *Coastal Journal* magazine. I poured myself a bowl of cornflakes and put the cereal box between us like a giant wall. Mom was rushing around making lunches, her wet hair still wrapped in a towel. She looked at the clock.

"Hey, I have to get ready. See you girls at the Laun-dromArt this afternoon. Have a great day at school." She rushed toward the bathroom, and then quickly turned. "Gale, we'll talk later."

All day at school the "Tide" song was playing in my head. I didn't realize I was humming until Mr. Elliot called on me.

"Gale? Would you like to share that song with the class?"

"Song? Oh. No. Sorry."

"Well, do you have an answer?"

"Answer?"

"Your author? Everyone is announcing their author picks today."

"Oh, yes, well, it's…" My brain stalled. I couldn't remember the author I was going to pick. I've read a million books. Why couldn't I think of one author? Then a name came to me.

"Miles Cassidy."

"Mmmm." Mr. Elliot slowly repeated the name. "Miles Cassidy. Don't know him."

"You said we didn't have to stick to your list, right?" I asked.

"Right. Well, I'm looking forward to learning more about your author tomorrow."

"Tomorrow?"

"Yes, Gale. Tomorrow. The first draft of the author bio is due."

"Right. I knew that. Tomorrow."

Whoops. I *didn't* know that. How did I miss the assignment? Easy. The heart stones.

After class, Celia found me in the hall. "Miles Cassidy? Why does that name sound so familiar?" she asked.

"That library book at Phoebe's house? Miles Cassidy wrote it. I think it was a poetry book. I can't remember the title. Can you?"

"Nope. I'm lucky I can remember my own homework. I picked Gertrude Chandler Warner. She wrote the Boxcar Kids books. I wrote a stage monologue biography last night. I'm acting it out."

"Sounds great. Well, you're way ahead of me!" I hurried down the hall. "See you later. I won't be in study hall. I have to go to the school library and do some research, quick!"

As soon as I got to the library, I Googled "Miles Cassidy." The first thing that popped up was a short biography:

> Born in Bangor, Maine, on July 25, 1870, Miles Cassidy had earned early success as a talented author, publishing two books of poetry: Trumpet Sounds (1895) and Footsteps (1898). Both books, originally released by Blue Seacoast Press, eloquently expressed Cassidy's love for Maine and its coastal landscapes. His timeless poetry has been shared and reprinted many times over the years. Mr. Cassidy was an English professor at University of Maine, Orono, for two years. On August 6, 1899, his life was cut tragically short when he was among 20 people killed in a ferry boat disaster in Bar Harbor, Maine.

Wow. What is it about boat disasters around here? I dug deeper and discovered more information on the accident and his family, and uploaded a few pictures. I printed everything, then went to the shelves to search for his books. I was surprised that the library had both of them. I looked closely at the book covers. *"Trumpet Sounds,* Poems by Miles Cassidy." That was the one! The book I saw at Phoebe's house.

TWELVE

After school, Emma and I walked through town in silence. This time, my headphones made a perfect "not talking to my sister" disguise.

As soon as we entered the LaundromArt, Emma headed to the back office. I looked for Mom and spotted her in the studio chatting with Mrs. Dalton from the Art Association. This wasn't good. Mrs. Dalton's stories were always dull, just like her paintings. Mom was trapped and probably bored to death.

I rolled the rack of clothing marked "dry cleaning" up to the front counter, slipped on my disposable gloves, and went to work emptying pockets. Suddenly, I heard a high-pitched grinding noise. I followed the sound.

There was Captain, lying on the floor, his head halfway under a washing machine.

"Hi, Captain."

"Hey, Windy. I didn't even hear you come in."

"I heard you," I said.

"What's the latest?"

"Okay. Wait till you hear this." I sat on the floor next to Captain's toolbox. "I called Phoebe about the song. You're not going to believe this. That song was *her* song, I mean, Pierre's song. Pierre sang it to Phoebe every time he went out to sea. And Pierre's father did the same. It's an old family song."

"Wow. Amazing."

"It's a clue." I leaned in closer. "Captain, can you take Celia and me out to sea on your boat?"

Captain scooted forward and sat up, wiping his greasy hands on a grimy rag. "Why?"

"The song's lyrics: *Follow your heart into the sea.* We have to go. We have to search."

"Windy, 'the sea' is a big place. Where do we even begin to look? And what are we looking for?"

Just then, I heard the bell over the door jingle. I jumped up and looked toward the front of the shop. My dad was walking in just as Mrs. Dalton was walking out.

"Hey, Dad. What are you doing here?" I went over to the front counter and gave him a peck on the cheek.

"Hi, Gale. I…I came to see you."

"Me?" Dad looked serious. I was trying to think fast.

What did I do? Emma probably opened her big mouth about something. Maybe our screaming match on the street.

"I need to show you something." Dad slipped his backpack off his shoulder, plopped it on the counter, and unzipped the front compartment. He shoved both hands into the pocket and pulled out handfuls of stones: heart stones. The stones clattered loudly as they hit the slate counter.

"*What*? Where?" A cluster of glistening pink heart stones looked up at me from the gray-blue countertop as if they were little fish in a pond, waiting to be fed.

"I found them lined up on the edge of the dock this morning," explained Dad.

"Wow. All of them?" I ran my fingers over the stones, quickly counting them. Twenty.

"Yup. And the dock, well, I found the stones on the exact dock where Pierre used to moor his boat."

"No way!"

The crash of the stones, the sight of my dad, and the mention of Pierre were enough to bring Mom, Emma, and Captain to the front counter.

"What's going on?" asked Mom.

"Dad found all these heart stones on the pier where Pierre moored his boat!"

"Okay. You are both freaking me out," said Emma. "Dad, please tell me you are not believing Gale's fairy tale? Things just don't appear. Someone put them there."

"It's not a fairy tale!" I said.

"Oh, come on!" Emma shook her head.

"Hang on there, Einstein. Let's hear them out," said Captain.

"Well, you're half right, Emma," said Dad. "I do think someone put them there, but that's not all. The tips of the hearts were all pointing in the same direction. Northeast."

"Okay? So what?" said Emma. "Someone just lined them up that way."

"There's more," said Dad. "When I picked up one of the stones and then put it back on the dock, it spun around until it was, again, pointing northeast."

"The same thing happened to me!" I said.

"What? It did? When?" asked Mom.

"At the library," said Captain.

Mom eyed Captain with a *how did you know that?* look.

"Yes. The library," I explained. "The heart stone spun around and pointed to some books on the shelf."

"You guys are talking crazy." Emma just wouldn't give up.

"I thought I was seeing things myself," said Dad. "But I'm telling you, it's true. I moved five different stones, and each one spun and stopped exactly at fifty degrees northeast. The stones must have some kind of strange magnetic energy."

"Fifty degrees northeast from South Harbor? That brings you toward the Ledges," said Captain.

"I told you, Dad! These stones have mystical powers." I hugged Dad, burying my face into his flannel shirt.

"Let's back up, Gale," said Mom. "The library? Twirling stones? The books? Why don't I know any of this?"

"I've been trying to tell you, Mom, but something always got in the way." I looked at Emma, then continued, "Mrs. Rosina, the librarian, found a heart stone on a shelf in the travel section. When I picked up the stone and put it back on the shelf, it started to *spin* and when it stopped, it was pointing at two books, one about the Maine islands and another about tides and currents. I have them at home."

I pulled my detective notebook out of my backpack. "Celia and I have been doing research. Read this."

I opened the page where I pasted the photo and description of Red Quartz.

I handed the notebook to Mom.

Mom's eyes widened as she read. She picked up one of the stones and peered at it closely. "That's incredible."

She looked at Dad, who was reading over her shoulder. He read the last line out loud: "Known to have mystical powers, this stone absorbs energy and guides toward the truth."

"These rocks are trying to lead us somewhere," I said.

"Gale, I think you're right," said Mom.

I could not believe that those words just came out of Mom's mouth.

"You're all nuts!" said Emma. She picked up one of the heart stones. "I feel absolutely nothing."

"Maybe you have to believe," I said.

"And I suppose next you are going to tell me Phoebe DuPont is a wizard!"

"Wait. What does this have to do with Phoebe?" asked Dad.

Dad was really behind the times. I flipped to the first page in my notebook. "We found eight other stones." I showed Dad the timeline and explained how all eight stones were left by Phoebe on Friday. I then told my parents the whole story about the flowers, the endless chowder, the song, everything.

"Are you sure it was Phoebe?" asked Dad.

"Yes. On Wednesday Celia and I went with Captain to return her coat and we talked to Phoebe for a long time. They *are* her heart stones. She has been finding them on her cove since right after Valentine's Day. So far she has collected over fifty heart stones."

Dad started pacing. "I'm guessing Phoebe made a trip to South Harbor yesterday. Wait. Let me find out." Dad stepped into Mom's studio and got on his cell phone. After a few minutes he returned.

"Yup. She was there. Mac said Phoebe dropped by the fishing shop yesterday to pick up some of Pierre's rods. Pierre dropped them off in December to be repaired. I asked Mac if Phoebe was walking anywhere near Pierre's dock. He said she was milling around for a while, but he wasn't paying too much attention. It had to be her." Dad paused. "I agree. These stones are pointing us some- where, somewhere beyond the harbor. But where are they coming from?"

"Phoebe is convinced that Pierre has somehow been sending the heart stones to her," I said.

"Pierre? How can that be?" asked Mom.

"She thinks Pierre is sending messages from heaven… But…" I cleared my throat. "But I…I think Pierre is alive and maybe Carlos too!"

Everyone stared at me. It was the first time I had been brave enough to say what I had been thinking.

"Alive? I don't know, Windy. Now that *would* be magic," said Captain. "Pierre and Carlos have been missing for a month, and the coast guard has searched and searched. I know those waters better than I know my own kids, and there's no way anyone can survive out there."

"We have to follow the clues," I said. "We have to go find them! Maybe they're hidden on an island. Maybe the coast guard missed them. There are three thousand one hundred sixty-six islands off the Maine coast. I've been reading."

"There sure are a lot of islands." Captain paused. "I tell ya, I've seen some strange things in my years, but nothing as strange as this. I just don't know how…"

"Please, Captain." I tugged on his sleeve. "You were

there. You listened to Phoebe. You heard all the stories. Maybe this is beyond logic. Maybe it is something that can't be explained."

Captain stroked his scraggly beard, and finally said, "Well, no harm in checking this out."

Mom looked surprised. "Really? You just said no one could survive…"

"Anna, I'm telling you, these stones have some kind of power." Captain turned to me. "Windy, let's take my boat out on Saturday morning. We'll take a spin around the coast."

I jumped into Captain's arms. "Thank you!"

"Now don't get your hopes up there, Windy," said Captain. "We might just be searching for snow in a desert. But either way, we need a plan. I'll go get my maps, and later I want to take a closer look at your books." Captain grabbed his coat. "And, Windy, you better let your sidekick know that we're heading out on the water bright and early Saturday morning." Captain started walking toward the door and turned. "Whoa, Nelly," he said, smiling. "I'm gonna have me a first and second mate!"

"Third mate. I'm going too," said Dad.

"Fourth! I'm coming," said Mom.

"Great golly! I got myself a crew!" crowed Captain.

Emma just rolled her eyes.

"Let's all meet at the house at six this evening to make a plan," said Mom.

"Great. See you then." Captain waved and headed out.

Dad ushered the pouting Emma toward the door. "We'll pick up pizzas," called Dad.

I couldn't believe it. My family was finally on board, and literally coming *ON* board! Well, everyone except Emma. I gathered the heart stones from the counter and put them in a bag. I looked at the clock. It was nearly closing time.

"Mom, can I invite Celia to dinner? She's been my Rockette, my partner, since the beginning."

"Sure. Call her. We'll walk by her house on the way home."

"Thanks, Mom."

When I told Celia about the twenty heart stones that Dad found at the pier, she dropped the phone.

"Did you say twenty?"

"Yes! Can you come over and…"

"I'll be there!" She agreed before I even finished my sentence. I told Celia about the boat trip we had planned for Saturday morning. She didn't even think twice.

"I'm in! I'm in!" she cheered.

"Okay, be on your porch in about ten minutes and I'll give you all the details."

"There's more?"

"There's more."

When we got home, Dad was already there, pouring root beer into pitchers of ice while Emma lined up the pizzas on the counter. Captain arrived soon after with an armful of maps.

After we gobbled up the pizza, I opened the *Currents and Tides* book while Captain spread out his enormous nautical map of the Maine coast. Mom, Dad, Celia, Captain, and I huddled around the table. I put a handful of heart stones in the middle of the map. "We need all the help we can get." I looked at Emma. She was on the couch with her nose in her computer, deep into her homework. We wouldn't be getting any help from her.

I took an orange highlighter and circled Hollow Point on the map. "So, all the heart stones have been washing up here."

Captain marked South Harbor and drew a line to the Ledge Islands. "I think we should start there, fifty degrees northeast of South Harbor."

"Can't be." We all turned. It was Emma.

"What can't be?" I asked.

"Currents," she said.

"What about them?"

Emma got up from the couch, bringing her laptop with her, and sat at the table. "Okay, I'll pretend that this is a scientific experiment…and I'll pretend that these heart stones actually washed in from the sea, and if all that were true, the stones wouldn't come from the Ledges."

Emma took a red pen and marked the map.

"The currents would have come from this direction. I've been studying the wind and tide data since the day of the storm. Now, I don't know exactly when these stones started washing up on shore, but you said Phoebe found the first one a few days after Valentine's Day. Right?"

I nodded. I was surprised she was listening.

"If that's the case, then the stones have been washing up on Hollow Point for a little over a month. Based on all the data, I'm thinking they are coming from the islands here." Emma circled a small group of dots on the map. "Ridge Islands. That's where we should look first."

"We?" I asked.

"Fifth mate...I'm coming too!"

After an hour, the plan was set.

"Okay then. See you all on Saturday morning, six o'clock sharp on the South Harbor docks. Looks like a great day for boating," Captain reported. "Calm seas, light breeze, clear skies. But it's going to be mighty chilly. It will be forty-five degrees on land. Lot colder in the sea. Bundle up."

Captain rolled up his maps, tipped his hat, and headed to the door. "And eat light."

THIRTEEN

It was Friday, just one more day until our heart stone ocean island search. This had to be the longest week of my life. Being a detective and a student was hard work. I got up early to write the draft of my biography, due today. Nothing like waiting until the last minute. I took out the Miles Cassidy poetry books and the research papers from my backpack and spread everything on my already crowded desk. As I thumbed through *Trumpet Sounds*, I couldn't help but think of Phoebe. There had to be a reason why she ended up with this book. I read a few love poems. They reminded me of the love Phoebe had for Pierre. I still thought that she should be coming with us on this search to find him. Last night, while we were making our plans, I asked Captain if we should ask Phoebe to come along and he didn't think it was a good idea.

"Windy, we don't want to get her hopes up," Captain said. "She seems to have finally accepted the fact that Pierre is gone. Just wouldn't be right. Best to keep this from Phoebe and the Sanchez family for now. Let's see how it goes."

I suppose Captain was right. We couldn't build them a pile of hope and then have it come crashing down.

When I saw Celia in the hall before English class, I pulled her aside. "Now remember, don't say anything to anybody about our trip tomorrow. It can't get back to Josie."

"Got it. Top Secret," said Celia, putting her fingers to her lips and making a *zip* motion.

We took our seats in class. I watched Celia turn to chat with Tory. I really hoped Celia was keeping it zipped. The last time she promised "Top Secret," she ended up showing a heart stone to Mrs. Rosina at the library.

Mr. Elliot collected the first drafts of the authors' biographies. *Check.* Amazingly, I finished just in time.

"Your final report is due on Tuesday," Mr. Elliot instructed. "Anyone who is planning an oral report, please pick a time slot and write your names on the board."

About half the class lined up to add their names to the list. I was sticking to a written report, but I couldn't even think about my English project right now. My school mind was as muddy as the soccer field.

Celia and I dragged ourselves through the school day, half listening to the teachers and half dreaming about an island rescue. Finally, it was the end of science class, the last period of the day. As we began to walk out of the classroom, Miss Howard stopped us.

"Celia and Gale? May I speak with you for a minute?"

I looked at Celia. Miss Howard must have noticed that our heads were not into frog anatomy. We both walked toward the front to the room while the rest of the class filed out. Miss Howard opened her desk drawer.

"I think this may be yours?" She placed a heart stone in the middle of her desk.

"Umm, might be," I said.

"I'm wondering, girls...I was in the library yesterday afternoon and Mrs. Rosina handed me this stone and said that another one of my students must have left it behind while researching my 'science project.' Now, I don't recall assigning a project? Do you?"

Celia was just about to speak, but I jumped in.

"It's a game. A treasure hunt," I said quickly.

Celia looked at me. "Yup. Treasure hunt."

I talked fast, before Celia could say a word. There was no way this heart stone mystery could leak out, not now, not right before tomorrow's search.

"It's an online game. You have to find the heart stones. It's fun."

"But why would you tell Mrs. Rosina that it was a science project?"

"Oh, it was part of the game. We wanted to throw off the other hunters. Sorry, Miss Howard."

"Hmmm. Well, okay." Miss Howard looked at the stone. "It is quite different."

"It's Red Quartz!" Celia blurted out.

I nudged her.

"Really? Maybe you can tell us more about it when we get to the geology unit."

"Sure," said Celia.

I tugged the back of Celia's sweater. "Sure thing. Miss Howard," I said. "We have to go now. Umm, Celia has piano lessons, and I have to get to my mom's LaundromArt."

"I don't…" began Celia. She looked into my wide eyes. "Yes. Piano. Right. Gotta run!"

"Well, here. Take the stone." Miss Howard dropped the heart stone into my hand. "And by the way, in case you are interested, Mrs. Rosina said to tell you she found the stone in the poetry section."

"Great." I poked Celia and we dashed toward the classroom door. "Thanks, Miss Howard."

We walked quickly down the hall with our lips clenched shut as we passed crowds of kids at their lockers. As soon as we were alone outside, I burst like a balloon. "The poetry section! It fits! Phoebe placed this heart stone on the shelf, and it must have pointed to the Miles Cassidy book!"

"That book is definitely another clue," said Celia.

The heart stone radiated a warm feeling in my hand, like the comfortable feeling you get when you find a true friend. I looked at Celia and smiled. "Tomorrow is the big day. See you in the morning. We'll pick you up at five forty-five."

"I'll be ready," said Celia.

Ready or not, this mystery was about to be solved. I hoped.

FOURTEEN

I woke up before the sun, too excited to sleep. I turned on my lamp and quietly began dressing in layers. Mom said, "Think snowstorm." That's what I did. Long underwear, jeans, shirt, a heavy sweater, fleece jacket, and wool socks. I dug out my favorite hat, gloves, scarf, and hooded raincoat with the deep front zip pocket. I packed my backpack with an extra pair of socks, binoculars, and my notebook, which I put in a waterproof bag. Last but not least, the heart stones. There was no way I'd take this trip without them. I opened the top drawer of my dresser. With the twenty stones that Dad found, the orange woolen sock was now crammed with heart stones. I added one more—the heart stone from Miss Howard—

and secured the sock with a few elastic hair ties. I placed the bulging sock in the front pocket of the backpack. I was about to close the drawer when I noticed the card, the card I'd made over four weeks ago. I ran my fingers over the bright painted rainbow and then tucked the card in the pocket of my fleece. Just as I was about to open my bedroom door, I came face-to-face with my calendar. Today was March 21st, the first day of spring. I flipped the calendar page back to February and counted. It had been thirty-four days since the Valentine's Day nor'easter. Could someone survive for thirty-four days in the sea? Mom always said that spring was a time for new beginnings. I hoped she was right.

The window at the top of the stairs looked out over the ocean. A sliver of light shone on the horizon. The sky above it was like a giant, dark stage curtain preparing to rise. I lifted my backpack over my shoulder. The show was about to begin.

Captain and Dad were already on the boat when we arrived. The sunrise welcomed us with a spectacular orange-and-pink-painted sky. Mom and Emma climbed aboard, while Celia and I lingered on the dock, looking out to the sea with wonder and hope.

"Well, I guess this is it," I said, squeezing Celia's hand.

As we boarded the *Crosswinds*, the boat began to rock from side to side. Dad looked at my face.

"It will get smoother when we get going," he said, reaching for my arm.

I held the railing to steady myself. "I just hope I don't lose my breakfast before we even leave the dock."

"You'll be fine," said Mom. "Breathe deep and look straight ahead."

With our life jackets on and gear stowed in a small compartment in the cabin, we were ready to go.

"Let's balance out the boat," said Captain. "Celia, Emma, and Gale, sit port. Anna and Ben, starboard."

Luckily, I had learned from Emma that port was the left side of the boat and starboard was right. Soon, the engine revved up, and we were off.

As planned, we first headed to Ridge Islands to follow up on Emma's scientific calculations. Forty minutes later we were thirty miles off the coast. Captain slowed the boat and we cruised around a group of ten tiny islands. Some were so small that they didn't look like islands at all, more like giant boulders floating in the sea. Captain told us to look for any signs of life: smoke from a campfire, a shelter, boat wreckage, and of course, Pierre and Carlos. We got as close as we could and slowly scanned the islands through our binoculars. Nothing.

"Okay. All clear," Captain called from the cabin. "We'll head to the Ledges. "Hang on, everyone. We're going to make some time."

The boat picked up speed and so did the wind. I doubled up my hood and burrowed close to Celia. I glanced at Emma. She looked disappointed, like she just got a big fat F on a project.

"It's okay," I said.

"You're not going to find them," said Emma. "They would have been there."

I hoped she was wrong.

Once at the Ledges, Captain once again slowed the boat, and we all got out our binoculars. Slowly, we circled twenty small islands and islets. Each time we passed on to the next island, I could feel the mood on the boat sink lower and lower.

After an hour, Captain said, "Sorry, Windy. There's nothing out here. We're heading back. That's it."

As the engine roared, Dad put his arms around me. "I'm sorry, honey."

I began to cry. "It can't be *it*." Mom, Celia, and even Emma joined us in a giant hug. Our tangled scarves danced in the billowing wind as we stood on the deck, huddled nose to nose. Then Celia began to sing: "*The Tide of Love Brings you back to me…*" Emma joined in, then Dad, then Mom, and finally me…"*Follow your heart into the sea.*"

I jumped back. "That's it! *The heart stones!*" I hurried to the storage compartment in the cabin, grabbed my backpack, and took out the woolen sock. I quickly removed the elastics, stood in the middle of the deck, and emptied out all the heart stones.

"Gale! What?" Mom was startled.

The heart stones hit the deck like hail falling from the sky. They bounced, clattered, and rolled until they finally settled.

Then it happened.

We all stepped back in amazement. The heart stones began to spin and turn until the tips of the hearts were all facing the same direction.

I hurried inside the noisy cabin, tugged on Captain's coat sleeve, and pointed to the back deck. "Captain—the heart stones! Turn the boat around!" I yelled. Captain took one look at the heart stones and began to steer the boat. Each time the boat changed direction the heart stones moved as one, like a single arrow on a magical compass.

"Well, I'll be!" cheered Captain.

As the boat sped along, Dad stood over the heart stones, calling out directions. We all sat in absolute astonishment as we watched the heart stones slowly turn in unison to guide the boat. I looked at Emma, who was as still as the fisherman statue. Her stunned face was white, jaw opened, eyes locked. Then she started yelling out directions too.

"Dad, the stones are moving to the right—the right— northeast!"

The heart stones directed the boat farther northeast than Captain had thought to go. Captain cruised along for thirty minutes, continuing to be guided by the heart stones. At this point, Celia, Emma, and I spread the Maine coastal map across our laps. It took all six hands to hold it down so it wouldn't blow into the sea. I called out the island names as we passed them. "That's Porcupine Island, starboard. Goose Island, port side."

Over the roar of the engine, Dad loudly called out the directions to Captain.

"Now keep straight," Dad directed.

"Are you sure?" asked Captain. "Looks like shallow water ahead of us."

Suddenly, the ocean got rough, rocking the boat and then tossing it violently. With a jolt Mom was thrown off the bench onto the deck. I grabbed Mom's arm to help her up when the boat pitched to the left, hurling Mom and all the heart stones port side.

"Hold on!" Captain gripped the steering wheel. "Feels like the currents are turning and churning."

"Tidal jets!" called Emma.

"What?"

"Tidal jets!" Emma said louder. "They're powerful reversing currents. That's what caused these big banks of sand. We need to go around them!"

"But the heart stones were guiding us northeast," Dad said, pointing.

"We can't go northeast!" called Captain. "Too dangerous. Emma is right. We need to go around the banks."

Just then a huge wave crashed into the boat, filling the deck with swirling water, washing the heart stones to the opposite side. Another wave hit; this time the heart stones splashed up in the air.

"We're going to lose the heart stones!" I yelled.

With Mom on the bench holding on for dear life, Dad, Celia, and I sank to our knees to collect the heart stones. It was like trying to round up balls on a moving pool table. Meanwhile, Emma and Captain were at the wheel, holding the maps between them.

"Head forty-five degrees north of west. Steer three hundred fifteen degrees," she yelled.

"Got it!" said Captain.

Somehow, working together, we managed to capture the heart stones and put them safely inside the now drenched woolen sock.

"We got them all," I said, clutching the sock full of stones. We plopped on the bench and took a collective breath. The boat was finally in calmer waters.

"Your sister is pretty smart," said Celia as we watched Emma help navigate the boat. "She sure knows a lot about tides."

"Lucky for us…right, Mom?" I turned to look at Mom. "Mom?" She was green. "Uh-oh. Are you okay?"

"I'm fine," Mom mumbled.

"You don't look fine," said Dad.

She wasn't. I was the one who usually got sick. This

time it was Mom. She hung her head over the side, and that was that.

Then suddenly word from the front. "Coming up to some rough waters. Not out of the woods yet!" Emma yelled. "I'll tell you when you can start using those heart stones!"

With the roar of the engine, the howling of the wind, and the nauseating sound of Mom barfing, we couldn't hear a thing.

I yelled to Dad, "What did she say?"

"She said we are out of the woods—start using the heart stones!" he yelled back.

"Okay!" I called.

I got up with the woolen sock. The boat jolted. I gripped the railing trying to steady myself, when suddenly *CRASH!* A wave. I looked at Mom. She was heading face-first into the water. In an instant, I grabbed the back of her coat and pulled her onto the deck, not even realizing that I let go of the woolen sock. I watched in horror as the sock flew out of my hand and into the air.

"*NOOOO!*" I screamed.

Everyone, including Emma and Captain, turned and looked up, following my gaze.

As if in slow motion, the sock sailed through the sky, then hit the water with a powerful splash. We all watched helplessly, as the orange sock, filled with precious heart stones, bubbled out of sight.

I slumped on the bench, defeated. "It's over."

"It is not over!" Emma was at my side. "Gale, we are absolutely *not* giving up! We just have to get back on course. I marked our location before we hit the tidal jet." She showed me the map. "Once we get around these shallow sand banks, we'll head northeast, back in the direction that the stones were pointing."

I followed her red marker line with my eyes as she spoke, reading all the island names on the course. My eyes jumped!

"That's *it*!" I screamed, pointing to the map. "Trumpet Island." I was standing now, yelling into the wind. "Captain—*TRUMPET*. Remember? The title of that book at Phoebe's house…*Trumpet Sounds!* It was a clue…it's the name of an island!"

Emma and Captain maneuvered the boat around the banks. The seas were now calm as we got back on course, heading to Trumpet Island.

"I see it! That must be it! I see the island. " I called as a small island came into view.

As we approached, Captain slowed the boat and we all stood up. From a distance the island didn't look much bigger than the Town Green. Clumps of evergreen trees and huge boulders bordered its shores. I saw a flash of color and grabbed my binoculars. It was something bright red, but I couldn't quite make it out.

Captain cut the motor. "Did you hear something?"

He turned the engine off completely. The boat drifted forward. "Quiet, everyone," he said.

Suddenly the stillness of sound was interrupted.

"*OVER HERE! HERE! We're here!*"

"Someone is yelling!" said Captain excitedly.

I peered through my binoculars, panning the shore. "I see two people! It's them! It's them!"

"It *is* them!" Dad yelled, still looking through his binoculars.

I burst out crying, falling onto the bench seat, overwhelmed with joy and disbelief. I looked up at Mom. "Mom? Am I dreaming?"

Mom sat next to me, rocked me in her arms, and kissed my head. "No, Gale. This is real." Mom pulled Celia and Emma onto the seat and gave us all a bear hug. "I can't believe it. You did it, girls. You found them."

The boat jerked and picked up speed. Dad was still standing with his binoculars to his face. "I see them waving!" said Dad. "And to the right looks like pieces of their red-and-white boat."

We all started cheering.

Emma was on her feet, jumping up and down. "We see you! We're coming!"

Captain tooted his horn and headed straight to the island's shore. "*YAHOO!* By golly, Windy. You girls did it!"

Celia and I looked at each other and smiled through our tears. We both knew it wasn't us; it was the heart stones and their undeniable magical power. We looked up into the bright blue sky, letting the sun warm our faces. One lone puffy white cloud hovered above Trumpet Island...and wouldn't you know...it was in the shape of a heart.

FIFTEEN

We pulled into the gravel driveway. Tulips lined the walkway. A welcome to spring, now, a welcome to life. Pierre jumped out of the truck before it even came to a complete stop and quickly dashed into the house, his house.

While Captain, Celia, and I got out of the truck, we heard a shatter of glass and a piercing shriek. We rushed to the door, only to find Pierre and Phoebe, on their knees, in a loving embrace, a blue broken teacup next to them on the floor. Tears flowed from Phoebe's eyes. She was nose to nose with Pierre, holding his bearded face in her hands, repeating, "You are alive. You are alive."

We stood in the hall in silence, our watery eyes watching this remarkable reunion. The answers to the questions *How? What? Where?* were suddenly unimportant. The only thing that mattered right now was that Pierre was home.

Suddenly, Phoebe jerked her head back with a panicked look. "Carlos! Where is Carlos? Is he. . . ?"

"Phoebe, Carlos is alive." Pierre gathered Phoebe once again into his arms. "It's okay, shh…we are both safe."

"Phoebe, my parents and sister are driving Carlos home right now." I smiled as I imagined the amazement and shock on Josie's face.

"Thank the stars!" Phoebe looked into Pierre's eyes. "Well, Captain, I have to admit, this is one of your best deliveries yet!"

"I'd have to agree!" laughed Captain.

"That's for sure!" cheered Celia.

Pierre and Phoebe got up from the floor and gathered everyone together in a giant hug. "Let's bring this hug-fest inside," said Pierre, with one arm over Captain's shoulder.

"Are you sure? "I asked, looking down at our clothes. "We're a sea-soggy mess."

Pierre laughed as he plucked a piece of seaweed from my hair. "I just spent a month in the middle of the ocean. Do you think I'm worried about a little sand and water?"

"A month! Dear me, Pierre, you must be starving." Phoebe scurried to the kitchen. "You go get washed up and into dry clothes and I'll heat you up some stew."

"And we'll get a fire going," said Captain.

Celia and I got some wood from the porch and by the time Pierre returned, the stew was hot and the fire was crackling.

We all settled around the table, with Phoebe clutching Pierre's arm. He looked at us with tired blue eyes.

"How?" he asked.

There was a long pause. I looked at the windowsill, then at Captain. He nodded. I slowly reached into the jar and placed a few heart stones in the middle of the table. "We followed the heart stones."

"Heart stones?" Pierre looked confused.

Phoebe squeezed Pierre's hand and looked up. "We can't explain how or why, but these heart stones have been washing up on our cove for weeks. I found the first one a few days after Valentine's Day. These two amazing girls put it all together. They followed clues and somehow figured it all out. They did it…Captain, too. And now you are here." Phoebe leaned her head on Pierre's shoulder.

Pierre looked astonished. He rubbed one of the stones and looked at Phoebe. "You know, the rocks around Trumpet Island were deep pink just like this. When I first noticed them, I thought about how you love to collect unusual stones, so each and every day I'd pick one up and say, 'I love you, Phoebe,' kiss it, and throw it into the sea. I was hoping and wishing that somehow my love would get to you."

"And it did," said Phoebe, smiling.

Pierre turned to us. His voice began to quiver, "What can I say? *Thank you* just doesn't seem like quite enough. I feel like I'm in a dream…a very good dream. You brought us home. I don't quite understand how all this came together, but—"

"You know, Pierre," interrupted Captain. "The story of the heart stones *is* pretty unbelievable. There were lots of twists and turns."

"And waves…lots of waves," cheered Celia.

"And guitar cases, and songs and flowers and chowder, and the dry-cleaning of a certain red coat, and books, and…" I started to giggle.

"Wow! I have *a lot* of catching up to do!" said Pierre.

"You sure do! But the thing is, it was Phoebe who brought you home! If she hadn't found the heart stones and pushed us to follow them, none of this—" My words were halted by a sudden knock on the door.

Pierre wiped his eyes and lumbered to the hall.

A small woman in a big fur leopard hat pushed herself through the door, into the house. "Well, I'll be! It's *true!*" she cried out.

As soon as she turned, we all recognized her. It was Edith Styles from the *Cliff Cove Times*. Everyone in town knew Edith, whether they wanted to or not.

"Hi, Edith." Pierre stepped back as Edith barreled into the room. "Ahh—come on in."

"Word sure spreads fast!" said Captain.

"You betcha! Small town, big news," said Edith. "Mac from the Fish and Tackle Shop saw you all at the dock. He called his wife Sally at the bakery, and that was it! You know Sally. She's a gabber. Word is traveling through Cliff Cove like wildfire. The phone lines, or cell towers… or whatever you call 'em are burning up. But you know me, I need to get the facts, see you with my own two eyes! So here I am."

"You sure are," Pierre chuckled. "Why don't we all sit down?" Pierre pulled up a cushioned armchair to the table for Edith. She took off her big hat, revealing her bright red hair, reached into a giant lime green leather bag, and pulled out a notebook. She got right to it.

"Captain, I was told that Carlos called his mother from the dock, but she thought it was some kind of a sick joke and hung up on him!" Before Captain could say a word, Edith turned. "What about you, Phoebe? When did you hear about the rescue?"

"I just found out, just now, when Captain drove Pierre here."

Pierre chimed in. "No way I was going to call Phoebe. If she heard my voice on the phone, she would have probably dropped dead before I got home!" Everyone laughed.

"Well, I did speak with Mr. Sanchez," Captain chimed in. "He didn't believe me either and said he wasn't *going to* believe it until he saw Carlos walk through his front door."

"Can't say I blame him," said Phoebe. "There's got to be a lot of hugging and cheering going on in that house right about now!"

"It is certainly quite an astonishing turn of events." Edith posed her pen in her notebook. "So, Pierre, I need the scoop. How did you survive out there?"

"You know, this is a long story. We may have to do an interview another time. Just say, we ate a lot of fish and used what was left of our boat as shelter. I owe a lot to Carlos. He's one strong young man. But mostly, we never gave up hope. I just kept singing a song I learned as a boy, a song that always brought my father home, *The Tide of Love brings you back to me.* We had faith that we would get back to our loved ones." He snuggled up to Phoebe.

I looked at Celia. Our ears perked up. We knew that song well!

"That is lovely. And yes, I do want a longer interview, an exclusive." Edith turned to Captain. "People are saying that you are a hero. How did you find them?"

"Well, it wasn't me. It was these two girls right here," Captain said, beaming. "We've got ourselves the finest detectives in Cliff Cove!"

"These girls? Detectives?" Edith blinked, red lips pursed. "Really? Aren't you Anna Tremonte and Doug Henderson's daughter? I've seen you at the laundromat."

"Yes. I'm Gale, Gale Hope Henderson; this is Celia Shen."

"So, let me get this straight. You young girls are responsible for finding Pierre and Carlos? How did you do it?"

"Well, it's hard to explain. You see, it all started with stones...heart stones."

"Heart what?"

I turned to the windowsill and gasped. Everyone's eyes looked at me, and then at the jar, a jar now filled with ordinary gray beach stones.

"What is it, dear?" continued Edith.

"Oh, nothing. Just looking out at the sea. Umm. It looks like a storm..."

"Well, dear, let's stay on track. You mentioned something about a heart?" Edith asked.

"Yes. Heart." I tried to calmly recover. "We, umm, followed our hearts."

I looked at Phoebe. She smiled and nodded. "That's what we did. Right, Celia?"

"Right. We followed our hearts," repeated Celia. "And we had some really good luck and a lot of help."

"Yup. Lots of help. My sister Emma, she's a whiz at tides and currents," I said. "And Captain here, he knows the coastal waters better than he knows his own kids.

I guess you can say there were lots of heroes. It was a group effort!"

"Excuse me. Edith, the truth is..." Phoebe began.

I held my breath.

"It must be said that Pierre and Carlos would have never been discovered without these girls. Gale and Celia just never gave up. They were blessed with a special gift to see beyond reality. When everyone, including myself, was convinced that Pierre and Carlos weren't coming home, they thought differently. They restored hope in our lives and in our hearts and gave us all a reason to believe."

Edith scribbled away. "Great quote." Then she closed her notebook and stuffed it in her green bag. "Well, this was just wonderful. Thank you. Pierre, welcome home. Get some rest. I'm on my way to interview the Sanchez family. I'll see you all tomorrow."

"Tomorrow?" asked Pierre.

"Oh, you'll find out soon enough. The town is pulling together a huge homecoming celebration on the Town Green tomorrow at noon. Rest up and don't be late!"

Edith plopped on her leopard hat and rushed out the door. We stood there looking at each other in shared stunned silence, a mix of dazed confusion, exhaustion, and joy.

"The heart stones? I don't understand," I finally said.

"I think sometimes, things just can't be explained," said Pierre.

"Our hearts have healed, and love has come home. What else do we need to understand? The mystery is solved," said Phoebe, still clinging to Pierre's arm.

"Stones or no stones, hope has been restored in Cliff Cove!" said Captain. "It's hard to remember the last time we had a reason to celebrate."

With that, we grabbed our coats and headed out the door. "We'll see you tomorrow."

SIXTEEN

The next day at noon, under overcast skies, the sound of clanging pots, jubilant cheering, and beeping horns echoed through the streets. Clouds and threatening skies weren't going to put a damper on this celebration. Mom, Dad, Emma, and I joined the growing crowd walking toward the Town Green. At every corner, people merged, some carting kids and coolers, others pushing carriages or wheelchairs. The parade of people slowed as we funneled into the Town Green. Hand-painted signs lined the fence: WELCOME HOME PIERRE & CARLOS—WE LOVE YOU—HOPE FOUND. Yellow streamers hung from the trees, and excited chatter filled

the air…*It's a miracle!…Can you believe it?…I wonder how?*
At the top of the center path, standing proudly above
the crowd on its granite base, was the fisherman statue, once again surrounded by flowers, only this time the
flowers symbolized pure joy.

Just then, a Dolphin Diner catering van backed up
near the walkway. We watched as three long tables were
carried onto the Green and a big portable stove was set
up under a white tent. A smiling Mr. Wheeler lugged
huge pots to the tables. I spotted Celia with her sister.

"I'm so proud of both of you!" Angela gave me a big
hug and then quickly turned. "Gotta run! You two have
fun. It's fish chowder day again. On the house!"

The crowd thickened. Celia and her parents stood
shoulder to shoulder with my family, all to the right
of the walkway. A high-pitched screech from a cranky
speaker got our attention. Sam was on a makeshift stage
hooking up the sound system. I turned and spotted
Sally balancing a huge cake, followed close behind by
her bakery staff carrying coffee urns, plates, and cups.

"I guess we *are* having a party!" I said to Celia.

Suddenly, we heard a collective gasp. Everyone turned
toward the gate where Pierre and Phoebe were emerging
from Captain's black truck. Right behind them was a van
carrying the Sanchez family. Cheers and applause rip-
pled through the huge crowd, spreading like giant waves
as the guests of honor made their way onto the Town
Green. Phoebe, in her big red coat, walked arm in arm

with Pierre. A smiling Josie was glued to Carlos, tightly holding his hand, as if she were afraid that he might disappear again. His beaming parents followed, waving and trying to answer questions shouted by the curious crowd. They slowly made their way up the path, stopping every two feet for a hug or a handshake.

Josie spotted our families and pulled Carlos and her parents off the path, into the crowd. Her parents and Carlos went down the line, hugging our parents and Emma. Mr. Sanchez reached Celia and me and lifted us up with a huge smile.

Mrs. Sanchez leaned in. *"Gracias,"* she said softly.

Mr. Sanchez released us, stepping back to reveal Josie and Carlos. Josie's eyes watered and her lip quivered. "I…I…want…" She tried to speak but couldn't. The four of us hugged, closed our eyes, and cried.

Carlos, overwhelmed with emotion, stood back and wiped his eyes with the cuff of his sweatshirt. "I don't know how you did it, but I'm sure glad you didn't give up on us. I am so…" Carlos stopped mid-sentence and turned toward the stage.

"That song," he whispered.

The sound of music echoed through the Green. Sam was singing "The Tide of Love." By now, everyone in town was familiar with the song, but now each and every resident in Cliff Cove relished its meaning.

Captain appeared on the path, waving and coaxing Carlos and Pierre toward the stage. As a chanting, jubilant crowd ushered them along, Carlos turned to us, waved his hat, and yelled, "Thank you!"

Celia and I were making our way closer to the stage when I felt a tug on my sleeve.

"Kayla? Kayla! You're here!"

"Gale, Celia! I had to come. I got a bunch of texts last night. You guys are heroes! My parents and I drove up this morning for the celebration." Kayla leaned in. "You have to tell me everything. I'm hearing all kinds of stories from the class…magical heart stones? What's that about?"

"We will," I said as the three of us huddled together. "We'll tell you everything. You won't believe what you've missed! When are you coming back to Cliff Cove?"

"We're moving back on June fifteenth."

"Awesome." We all high fived. "We're going to have the best summer ever!"

From behind us, I heard my sister's voice, "Gale! Celia!" I turned to see Emma waving us over.

"Looks like your sister wants us," said Celia.

I looked at Kayla. "We'll be right back!"

We wiggled our way to where my family was standing. Captain was there too, sharing a laugh with Mom and Dad.

Emma's eyes shifted back and forth. "What's going on?" she asked in a hushed tone. "This little lady with a cat for a hat just came up to me, asking me about the rescue and telling me that *you* said I was a hero."

"Well, Emma, you *are* a hero," I said. "We wouldn't have made it to Trumpet Island without you. You knew about the tidal jets and the tides and helped us navigate around those sand banks."

"I guess we're a pretty good team after all!" Emma playfully nudged my shoulder and smiled. "A little bit of science mixed with a boatload of hope!"

Then Emma looked down. "But really, you two are the heroes. You never gave up, even when I told you your heart stone theory was nothing but a fairy tale."

"Maybe it was," I began.

"What do you mean?" asked Emma.

"I didn't want to tell you, but the heart stones... they've disappeared."

Mom heard what I said and chimed in. "Well, not really, Gale. They're at the bottom of the ocean."

"No, I mean the magic, it's gone." I went on to explain how the heart stones in the big jar at Phoebe's were now ordinary beach stones.

"That can't be," said Dad.

"Yup. Saw it myself. Nearly fell off my chair," said Captain.

"Gale is right," said Celia, reaching into her pocket. "I had one heart stone at home. This is it." She opened her hand and presented a dull, sand-colored common beach stone.

"Wait. This doesn't make sense. What about our card? And its bright rainbow painting?" asked Emma.

"The card! That's right!" I felt the pocket of my fleece. It was still there. I reached in and pulled it out. Emma looked over my shoulder. The rainbow on the card was back to its clouded, washed-out gray.

"Wow. It's almost as if this week had never happened," I said, slowly looking around. "But it did."

Just then, the crowd erupted into cheers. Under a gentle rain of confetti, Pierre and Carlos made their way onto the stage. As Pierre was about to take the microphone, a powerful gust of wind blew in from the ocean, right through the Town Green. As the trees swayed and the yellow streamers danced, my card was whipped from my hand. I watched it whirl and twirl toward the sky.

The crowd hushed as the sky brightened. Everyone looked up. Slowly the clouds parted, revealing a beautiful rainbow streaking across the blue sky. It was as if the wind had whisked away the last of the lingering gloom, leaving Cliff Cove once again filled with happiness and hope.

THE END

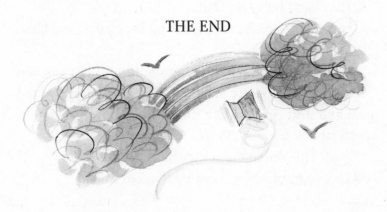

ACKNOWLEDGMENTS

Thank you to my talented writer-daughter, Kristin, for being my first reader and editor, and for supplying me with wonderful "middle-school teacher-eye" insights.

Sincere gratitude to my friend Jill Weber, book designer extraordinaire, who generously shares her creative wisdom.

And to Stephanie Mulligan, for believing in Heart Stones.